STARS IN THE SKY

In the drawing room he insisted Sylvia sit on the sofa beside him. He sat with his arm across the back of the sofa behind Sylvia. She was aware of his hand brushing against her shoulder. With sinking heart Sylvia saw that the clock in this room now said half past ten.

She knew she must bow to the inevitable and remain at Endecott for the night. She therefore broached the subject of the fire in her room with the Count. Would he please order Polly to light it?

"What, is my little chicken cold then?" The Count's words were slurred.

At this moment Polly came in with the coffee. Sylvia glanced at her before answering the Count.

"I find the red room cold, yes. It will be especially so by now."

Polly smirked as she leaned down to place the coffee before them. "You won't have no need of a fire, miss. Not with his lordship there."

Sylvia gasped in shock. The Count however merely threw his head back and laughed.

"That's enough now, Polly, you naughty girl!"

Polly glanced triumphantly at Sylvia and went out.

The Barbara Cartland Pink Collection

STARS IN THE SKY

BARBARA CARTLAND

Barbaracartland.com Ltd

First published on the internet in 2005 by
Barbaracartland.com

ISBN 1-905155-05-0

*The characters and situations in this book are entirely
imaginary and bear no relation to any real person or
actual happening.*

Printed and bound in Great Britain by CLE-Print Ltd. of St
Ives, Cambridgeshire.

THE BARBARA CARTLAND PINK COLLECTION

Barbara Cartland was the most prolific bestselling author in the history of the world. She was frequently in the Guinness Book of Records for writing more books in a year than any other living author. In fact her most amazing literary feat was when her publishers asked for more Barbara Cartland romances, she doubled her output from 10 books a year to over 20 books a year, when she was 77.

She went on writing continuously at this rate for 20 years and wrote her last book at the age of 97, thus completing 400 books between the ages of 77 and 97.

Her publishers finally could not keep up with this phenomenal output, so at her death she left 160 unpublished manuscripts, something again that no other author has ever achieved.

Now the exciting news is that these 160 original unpublished Barbara Cartland books are ready for publication and they will be published by Barbaracartland.com exclusively on the internet, as the web is the best possible way to reach so many Barbara Cartland readers around the world.

The 160 books will be published monthly and will be

numbered in sequence.

The series is called the Pink Collection as a tribute to Barbara Cartland whose favourite colour was pink and it became very much her trademark over the years.

The Barbara Cartland Pink Collection is published only on the internet. Log on to www.barbaracartland.com to find out how you can purchase the books monthly as they are published, and take out a subscription that will ensure that all subsequent editions are delivered to you by mail order to your home.

If you do not have access to a computer you can write for information about the Pink Collection to the following address :

Barbara Cartland.com Ltd.

240 High Road,

Harrow Weald,

Harrow HA3 7BB

United Kingdom.

Telephone & fax: +44 (0)20 8863 2520

THE LATE DAME BARBARA CARTLAND

Barbara Cartland who sadly died in May 2000 at the age of nearly 99 was the world's most famous romantic novelist who wrote 723 books in her lifetime with worldwide sales of over 1 billion copies and her books were translated into 36 different languages.

As well as romantic novels, she wrote historical biographies, 6 autobiographies, theatrical plays, books of advice on life, love, vitamins and cookery. She also found time to be a political speaker and television and radio personality.

She wrote her first book at the age of 21 and this was called *Jigsaw*. It became an immediate bestseller and sold 100,000 copies in hardback and was translated into 6 different languages. She wrote continuously throughout her life, writing bestsellers for an astonishing 76 years. Her books have always been immensely popular in the United States, where in 1976 her current books were at numbers 1 & 2 in the B. Dalton bestsellers list, a feat never achieved before or since by any author.

Barbara Cartland became a legend in her own lifetime and will be best remembered for her wonderful romantic novels, so loved by her millions of readers throughout the world.

Her books will always be treasured for their moral message, her pure and innocent heroines, her good looking and dashing heroes and above all her belief that the power of love is more important than anything else in everyone's life.

"To look at the stars in the sky at night is always exciting and romantic wherever your are in our world."

Barbara Cartland

CHAPTER ONE
1878

It was after ten o'clock in the evening, but carriages were still rolling up to the imposing house on Park Lane that was the residence of Lady Lambourne. As the front door opened to admit various tardy guests, strains of the latest fashionable waltz escaped into the crisp night air.

Lady Lambourne's annual masked ball was famous and everyone of consequence in London hoped for an invitation.

The ballroom inside was crowded. Tiaras sparkled under glowing chandeliers. Couples whirled elegantly about the dance floor, creating a melée of colours. The muslin drapes at the French windows billowed gently, ushering in a welcome breeze.

Sylvia, daughter of the Duke of Belham, had danced until she was dizzy. She was hoping to sit out the next waltz but here was yet another gentleman reminding her that his name was on her card. She rose with as much grace as she could muster.

If she sat out too many dances she knew her two sisters or her step-mother, the Duchess of Belham, would swoop on her with outraged cries. Her sisters, Edith and Charlotte, had both managed to secure husbands at the last ball. Now it was to be Sylvia's turn. The last thing Sylvia wished for, however, was a society husband.

Since her father, the Duke of Belham, had remarried some eight years ago, the family had lived in London. The new Duchess of Belham wished it that way. She had no desire to bury herself and her handsome step-daughters deep in the country, at the family seat of Castle Belham.

"Why, I'd simply die with all that silence!" she would cry when the Duke tried to coax her into spending a summer at the castle. "And when it isn't silent the noise is simply barbarous – cows and cockerels and dogs – and foxes howling in the woods. My darling husband, if you love me, you'll never ask me to disappear into the wilds like that."

The Duke would fall silent, for he did love the Duchess and he was grateful that she was such a conscientious step-mother. As he did not relish spending the summers alone, he remained with his family in London or on the Riviera, where the Duchess insisted they keep a seafront residence. It was on the Riviera that he had discovered the pleasures of the casinos.

His elder daughters Edith and Charlotte were delighted with their existence. They shared with their step-mother a love of town gossip, expensive hats, tea parties and balls.

Sylvia, however, longed for the country life. She greatly missed Castle Belham, where she had lived until the age of ten.

She remembered frosty mornings when she had run out to help the housemaid search for eggs. She remembered the bleating of lambs in the spring. She remembered lazy summer days when she sat in the boat-house, dangling her feet in the river. Days when the smell of new mown hay filled the air. She remembered most of all riding out with her father early in the morning, when the dew still glittered on the grass.

She and her father shared a passion for the country and for ancient Castle Belham.

Sometimes in London they rode out in Rotten Row, but it was not the same. There were too many other riders and one was rarely allowed to gallop.

Sylvia flinched as her latest partner dug his fingers into her waist. She stared resolutely over his shoulder as they slowly circled the floor. Oh, she was bored, bored with all this! Her satin shoes pinched her feet and her mask pinched her nose. She had danced with so many dull men who only wanted to indulge in light banter. Surely there was *someone* here, who had something to talk about other than Ascot or the latest singing sensation at Covent Garden!

At last the dance ended and Sylvia was led back to her seat. She sank gratefully onto the red velvet chaise and surreptitiously eased her feet out of her shoes. She exercised her ankles under her white dress, turning them first this way, then that.

"What are you doing, Sylvia?" came the simultaneous voices of her sisters. Sylvia looked up guiltily. Edith and Charlotte loomed over her. They were dressed respectively in red and jade, with matching masks through which their eyes glinted suspiciously.

"My feet are so tired," explained Sylvia. "I just had to take a rest."

"Have you kicked off your shoes?" demanded Edith incredulously.

Sylvia nodded.

"Oh, what *are* we going to do with you!" cried Charlotte. "Even after all this time in London, you still act like a country bumpkin! Don't you realise how lucky you are to be here? This ball is so popular, Lady Lambourne has taken to issuing only two invitations per family. *We* received *five*! We are highly honoured."

Sylvia sighed meekly. "Oh, I know, and I *am* grateful."

"Then why are you sitting here like a wallflower?" asked Edith.

"I promise you I have had ever so many dances."

"Ever so many is never enough!" declared Charlotte. "You have to dance with every gentleman who asks, because one of them just might be *the* one."

"Just think of how *we* persevered last year!" said Edith. "My feet were positively bleeding by the time Lord Rossington asked me to dance."

Sylvia was silent. She could not have borne to marry Edith's thin-lipped Lord Rossington, or the jowly Duke of Cranley whom Charlotte had ensnared.

The Duchess of Belham bustled up to her step-daughters. The feathers in her tiara bobbed officiously and Sylvia had to bite her lip to stop herself smiling at the sight. "There is a rumour that Lord Salisbury himself is here tonight," beamed the Duchess. "And guess who I caught a glimpse of in the adjoining salon?"

"Who?" breathed Edith and Charlotte simultaneously.

"The Prince of Wales! He's wearing a mask but there's just no disguising that girth, my dears!"

"We want to see, we want to see!" squealed Edith and Charlotte. Forgetting Sylvia entirely, they rushed off in excitement. The Duchess frowned down at her youngest step-daughter.

"Now you are getting about, aren't you? You're a very pretty gel, you know, and you must resist that tendency of yours to hide!"

"Yes, ma'am."

"Good, good. Well, I have promised a waltz to Lord Malmsbury. I had better go."

The Duchess sailed off in her voluminous blue gown.

Sylvia slid her feet back into her shoes and stood up. She caught sight of herself for a moment in one of the gilt mirrors that edged the ballroom. She supposed she was pretty, with her golden curls and her large blue eyes, but she rarely paid much attention to her appearance. Her sisters contended that were it not for her step-mother fussing over her wardrobe every morning, Sylvia would probably go about looking like a dairy-maid. The musicians struck up. Out of the corner of her eye Sylvia thought she saw her last partner bearing down on her again. No, she simply could not abide another dance! Without a backward glance she hurried over to the open French windows and passed through into the garden.

The fresh air was cool on her feverish cheeks. Tearing her mask from her face, she tripped across the terrace and down the steps onto the lawn. It was still March and not a warm night but Sylvia did not care. She had felt so imprisoned in that hot, noisy ballroom.

She stepped out of her shoes again and wriggled her toes in the damp grass. It was blissful. Then, shoes in hand, she flew down the garden, under the twinkling stars. The garden was one of the largest in London and she was breathless by the time she reached the fountain that stood at the bottom. Dropping her shoes, she stepped easily up onto the smooth encircling wall and walked dreamily around.

The stars above were mirrored in the water and looked like silver coins flung into a wishing well. Sylvia glanced back at the house – all lit up like a ship at sea – and then, lifting her dress gingerly, she dipped a foot into the fountain. How deliciously cool the water was! She dipped her other foot in. Heaven! She set up little waves with her toes that made the stars bob to and fro. As the water settled again, she noticed one star that shone with a particular brilliance. She stared hard at it, her head on one side.

"I wonder what *you* are called!" she mused aloud.

She gasped as a voice from the shadows answered her. "That is Arcturus, thePathfinder."

Dropping her skirts, Sylvia sat quickly down and groped with her feet for her abandoned shoes.

"Are these what you are seeking?"

A tall gentleman in a black mask stepped forward. Sylvia saw her shoes sitting on his outstretched palm.

"Why…yes. Thank you."

The gentleman gave a bow and then to Sylvia's consternation knelt before her.

"Put out your foot," he commanded.

Blushing a little, Sylvia did as he asked. Gently the mystery gentleman slipped on her shoes. His head bent before her, Sylvia noted dark brows and hair of a blue-black hue. At least, it seemed blue-black in the moonlight.

His task done, the gentleman straightened and regarded Sylvia gravely.

"I hope I did not frighten you?" he murmured.

Sylvia shook her head. "No…I was startled, that is all." The gentleman rose as if to depart but Sylvia rushed on. "I am glad you…answered my question…for it's a very beautiful star and it was a pity not to know its name. I'd rather talk about the stars than racing or hats…or whatever famous person has arrived at the ball. I came into the garden to get away from all that."

The gentleman smiled. "I rather did the same," he said.

"So do you know the names of any of the other stars?" asked Sylvia.

"Yes, I do," he replied simply.

"That one there, for example," Sylvia pointed. Her eyes shone brightly in the moonlight and her golden hair stirred in the breeze. Her companion gazed at her a moment before answering.

"Which one? Oh, yes, that is the polar star. And there

is the plough." He turned back to Sylvia. "Have you never been interested in the heavens before?"

"Oh," said Sylvia, ashamed. "I used to love looking at the stars and…wondering what else was up there…and what everything was called. But that was when I lived in the country. Since I've lived in London, I don't think about the sky so much. Most of the time it's hidden, by clouds or fog or…well, city air."

The gentleman smiled. "It is true, you rarely see the stars in all their glory here in London."

"How do you…know so much about them?" enquired Sylvia.

"Well, I am something of an amateur astronomer. I have a telescope at my home in the country."

"How fascinating!" exclaimed Sylvia. She kicked at the grass and then looked up at her companion shyly. "Do you…live in the country most of the time?"

"I do."

"Oh, how I envy you," she sighed wistfully.

"Not many young ladies envy a country life."

"But *I* do! I miss it terribly. And I miss our family seat, Castle Belham. Do you know it?"

"As a matter of fact, I do," began the gentleman.

"And do you know the legend of the lost treasure of Belham?" Sylvia ran on.

The gentleman smiled. "I have heard some rumours but I do not know the legend in full."

"Then I will tell it to you!" cried Sylvia triumphantly. "In return for you telling me all about the stars."

Her companion hesitated. "I shall be glad to hear it, but I should like to offer you my cape. I am concerned that you are sitting out here with no shawl."

"Oh, I don't need one," cried Sylvia airily. "I grew so

7

hot and bothered in there. I'm not cold at all. But I will accept your offer," she added quickly as she glimpsed a concerned frown forming on her companion's forehead.

Her companion removed his cape and slipped it around Sylvia's shoulders. Then he somberly sat down beside her to listen to her story.

"It all happened during the time of the Civil War. My ancestor, James, Duke of Belham, fought on the side of King Charles. When it became clear the Royalist cause was lost, he buried some of his fortune – jewels and gold nuggets – somewhere in the castle or castle grounds, and fled to France. There he enlisted in the services of the French King and was eventually killed in a skirmish against the French protestant rebels led by the Prince de Condé."

"And was the castle sequestered by Cromwell, when he came to power after the civil war?" enquired Sylvia's companion.

Sylvia shook her head. "No. Because, you see, the Duke's heir, his nephew, was a loyal Roundhead, and so Cromwell allowed him to keep everything."

"That is a most interesting story," said her companion.

"Yes, it is," nodded Sylvia. "I used to dream of finding the treasure when I was little, but I don't think I ever could have done as I don't really believe it exists. I think it was just a story circulated by the nephew to explain why so much of the property disappeared while the Duke was still alive, living in France. I think the nephew was a bad lot and he took the opportunity of the Duke's exile to sell things off."

Her companion was about to comment when a figure came out onto the terrace of the house and started to call. "Sylvia? Are you out there? If you are, you must come in at once. We are preparing to leave."

Sylvia leapt to her feet. "That's my step-mother. I

must go. I must go." She ran forward a few steps and then stopped in her tracks and whirled round. "Oh, your cape, I forgot." She hurried back and handed the cape to the tall, dark haired figure. "I really enjoyed talking to you…it was so much better than dancing with all those tedious society gentlemen! Good-bye, good-bye."

With a wave of her pretty, white hand she turned and raced away over the lawn.

The dark, masked gentleman watched her slender, retreating figure for a moment. Then, noticing something in the grass at his feet, he stooped to pick it up.

It was a delicate, gold trimmed white mask.

*

When Sylvia reached the terrace the Duchess greeted her crossly.

"Look at your dress! The hem is wet and covered in grass stains. Oh, you are hopeless! And who was that you were talking to out there?"

Sylvia glanced helplessly back at the fountain. The mysterious gentleman had gone but obviously the Duchess had seen him sitting there with her.

"I don't know," she admitted.

"You were out there on your own with a total stranger? Do you have no sense of propriety at all? What are we going to do with you?"

"I don't know," said Sylvia again, gazing down at the tips of her satin shoes. A sudden flush rose to her cheeks as she remembered the gentleman slipping them gently on to her feet.

"We shall have to send you away to finishing school," muttered the Duchess darkly. "Now your sisters and I are ready to leave, but we cannot find your father. Have you any idea where he is?"

"I could go and look," suggested Sylvia, anxious to

9

get away from the Duchess in her scolding mood.

"Yes, you do that, and tell him to hurry."

Sylvia slipped back into the ballroom through the French window. Couples were still gliding about the floor to the sound of a waltz, although when Sylvia looked at the musicians, they seemed ready to drop with exhaustion. She hurried out of the ballroom and into a wide corridor. Doors opened on to cosy drawing rooms where ladies sat chatting on vast sofas.

At the end of the corridor she came across the library. There was a great deal of cigar smoke in the air, firelight glinted on half empty bottles of port, and gentlemen sat hunched in expectation at a series of card tables.

Sylvia's heart sank as she recognised one of the hunched figures.

"Papa!" she murmured to herself sadly.

He had promised them all that he would gamble no more. He had lost so much money on their last visit to the Riviera. Sylvia moved swiftly forward and put a hand on her father's shoulder. He gave a guilty start.

"Why, Sylvia, I – I came in here to smoke a cigar, don't you know, and I was inveigled into making up a set."

"Yes, Papa," said Sylvia gently. She knew how hard he found it to resist the lure of a game. He was convinced he could win back all he had lost, if only his family would let him.

"Doing rather well, m'dear. If you could let me alone for another half hour or so."

"But Mama is ready to go," said Sylvia. "We are all ready."

"Perhaps," suggested the Duke weakly, "I could come on – later."

"No Papa, that's not a good idea. If you don't come with me, Mama will surely come to get you."

At the thought of the Duchess catching him at cards, the Duke rose hastily to his feet. He made his excuses to his partners in the game and followed Sylvia morosely to the carriage that awaited them.

*

The Duchess sliced off the top of her egg with a silver knife. "It's so hard to get a good duck egg, you know," she commented. "I'm very satisfied with these. I always send cook to Fortnum's to get them. Sylvia, won't you eat one?"

"Thank you, but I'm not really hungry."

The Duchess looked at her sharply. "You're spoiling for a cold, I'm sure. Sitting out in the garden last night without a shawl."

Sylvia hoped her step-mother was not right, but her throat did indeed feel rather raw this morning and she could not bear the idea of food.

"I don't know what I'm going to do with her, Charles," sighed the Duchess to her husband. "She danced only once with each of her partners last night. That is hardly giving them a fighting chance, is it?"

"Perhaps not, m'dear." The Duke pushed back his chair and rose from the table. "Well, if you'll excuse me, I must go and attend to my post."

The Duchess waved a hand. "Oh, I've told Carlton to bring the post in here to the breakfast room."

The Duke, who had been very quiet all through breakfast, sank back into his seat with a defeated air. As if on cue the door opened and Carlton came in with the morning's post and a letter opener on a tray.

"Your Grace," he said, depositing the bulk of the letters in front of the Duke before moving round the table to the Duchess.

The Duke regarded the pile in front of him gloomily. He picked up one letter, glanced at it, threw it down, and chose another. He slit the second envelope open and stared into it without removing the enclosed correspondence.

Sylvia watched him with concern.

The Duchess was examining a postcard that had arrived for her. "From Lady Frambury," she exclaimed. "She has gone to the Riviera already and says it's terribly pleasant. Perhaps we should consider travelling out at Easter."

The Duke did not seem to be listening. He put the second envelope down beside his plate and gazed into space.

"Did you hear me, dear?" said the Duchess.

The Duke looked absently at his wife. "What did you say, my darling?"

"I said, perhaps we should consider going to the Riviera earlier this year."

"I think – " said the Duke slowly, "that perhaps we should not. Fact is, m'dear we're – we're going to have to give up the house there."

"*Give it up?*" echoed the Duchess in astonishment. "But why?"

The Duke picked up the pile of letters before him and let them slide through his hands. "Here's why. Bills. Bills. And more bills. And I simply haven't the money to pay them. You may as well hear it before the bailiffs arrive."

The Duchess looked faint. "B…bailiffs?"

"Papa, you don't mean it, do you?" asked Sylvia in a low voice.

"I nearly do, m'dear. We've spent a great deal of money on our – London life, while the land at Castle Belham – has been neglected. The fields that used to be put to the plough and the cattle that used to graze there are all neglected. I never replaced the manager who used to collect the rents from the farms. We've been living beyond our means and if we don't tighten our belts – I'll be declared a bankrupt."

"And whose fault is that?" cried the Duchess. "Who lost thousands…yes, thousands…at the card tables in Monte Carlo?"

"I am at fault," agreed the Duke sadly. "But – just think of what all those parties and balls – all that gallivanting through the fashionable resorts on the Continent – have cost us in dresses alone."

The Duchess burst into tears. "Am I now to be blamed for trying to find husbands for your own daughters?"

"Hush, m'dear, hush. You have been a most admirable mother to my girls."

"And what about your favourite, Sylvia?" sobbed the Duchess. "How am I to find *her* a husband, if I can't spend tuppence ha'penny?"

Such a look of strain passed across the Duke's face that Sylvia was alarmed.

She rose swiftly from her chair and went to her father's side. "It's all right, Papa. I don't care much for shoes and hats and things. I don't mind wearing this season's dresses next year. And I really don't mind if I don't go to so many balls."

Her father took her hand and clasped it to his bosom. "Bless you, m'dear."

"She is impossible!" wailed the Duchess. "She'll die an old maid and it won't be for want of trying. I suppose she won't want a coming-out party next."

"I don't." said Sylvia stoutly.

Even the Duke shook his head at this. "Oh, now that's a thing – you must have one, no question. Every girl must have – a coming-out party. But it can't be held here, that is all."

"Where on earth can it be held, then?" demanded the Duchess.

"Why, at – Castle Belham," said the Duke.

Sylvia drew in her breath. There was nothing she would like more than to return to her childhood home.

The Duchess, however, was horrified. "Castle Belham? We might as well throw a party on the moon. Who would come? Red faced Squires and…and…ploughmen! No, no, I can't countenance it."

The Duke spoke wearily. "My dear wife, I am not as you know a firm man. I rarely ask you to do as I suggest. But I have to tell you, I sold my stocks and shares to finance Edith and Charlotte's weddings. I know I've been most improvident – I know it is my fault, but the fact of the matter is, the coffers are empty. We're going to have to shut up this house, until the situation improves. We're going to have to go and live at Castle Belham. It will be much cheaper to live in the country."

"I shall never be able to bear it!" shrieked the Duchess. She rose and with her handkerchief pressed to her lips, hurried weeping from the room.

The Duke slumped miserably in his chair. "My dear Sylvia – what have I brought upon us all?"

Sylvia barely heard. Her heart was pounding in her breast and a voice seemed to be singing in her head.

I'm going home, it sang. *I'm finally going home.*

CHAPTER TWO

Two weeks later, their London house shut up and most of the servants dismissed, the Duke and Duchess and Sylvia left for the country.

When their train pulled into the town of Norwich, the Belham family coach was waiting at the station.

The coach was something of a shock. The axles were rusty and the carriage caked with mud. The crest on the side of the coach had so weathered, it was barely visible. The driver wore no livery and there was no footman beside him on the box.

The Duchess pursed her lips but managed to hold her tongue.

The Duke put up a brave front as he gazed at the Belham coach.

"A lick of paint is all it needs," he said.

Sylvia felt sorry for her father, but she could barely repress her happiness at being on her way to Castle Belham.

She had not been sorry to leave the tall house in Mayfair where she had lived for the past eight years. She had never felt at home in its over-furnished rooms. Her father was too fond of the Duchess to question her taste in décor, which ran to such horrors as olive wallpaper and tartan sofas.

Sylvia had of course been sorry to say good-bye to

some of the servants and to Tilly, the kitchen cat, who was a superb mouser. She had even been sorry to say good-bye to her elder sisters. They had sobbed bitterly when the Duchess told them of the unfortunate downturn in the family's fortunes. They had begged the Duke not to exile himself at Castle Belham. Their husbands, however – Lord Rossington and the Duke of Cranley, both sober and far-sighted gentleman – were secretly relieved. They had no wish to start digging into their own pockets to keep the Belham household afloat in London. No, they argued, the Duke's decision to retreat to Belham was a sound one.

Sylvia had only one real regret at leaving London.

The night before her departure, she had knelt at her window gazing out at the quiet gardens and the night sky.

Arcturus, the Pathfinder, glittered brightly above the trees.

Looking at it, Sylvia had sighed.

Once secreted deep in the country, far from the round of parties and balls that defined London life, she had little chance of meeting her mysterious star-gazing gentleman again.

"No, no – put the larger one at the bottom!"

The Duchess was issuing loud instructions to the porters.

The driver remained on his box, whistling under his breath as the porters heaved up some of the heavy trunks. The rest of the luggage – including the hatboxes and calf - skin suitcases of the Duchess – would be sent on later.

The Duke handed his wife and his daughter into the carriage. They sank onto the dusty leather seats and the coach set off.

As the coach rolled out of town, Sylvia lowered the window and cried out excitedly at the view. The countryside wore all the gaiety of Spring. Buds were breaking on the trees, lambs were gambolling in the fields. The air was fresh and full of the scent of Spring flowers.

Castle Belham was a long way from the country town of Norwich and nearly three hours passed before the coach came to a halt before a pair of ornate gates. The driver whistled and the gate-keeper hurried out of his lodge.

"Oh, we still have a gatekeeper at least," said the Duchess bitterly.

The gates groaned on their hinges as the keeper heaved them open. He tipped his hat as the coach trundled through.

The drive was pitted with holes. A lot of trees on either side were cloaked in moss. The undergrowth was dense.

The coach had to halt at one point as three sheep ambled across its path.

"Whose sheep are those?" the Duke called up to the coachman.

"Them're yours, Your Grace," replied the coachman. "The fences round their field is rotten and broken through. They goes where they pleases."

"Hmmn," muttered the Duke to himself as he settled back in his seat.

At last the coach broke from the trees and drew up outside the castle. The Duke stepped out and then extended a hand to his wife and daughter.

"Oh my goodness!" exclaimed the Duchess.

The square stone castle looked horribly neglected. Ivy ran wild over the stone walls, covering some of the windows completely. Parapets had crumbled and the steps leading up to the front entrance were cracked. One of the ornamental lions that flanked the steps had lost its head.

"Tut tut," muttered the Duke. "It's rather more dilapidated than I had expected."

Sylvia blinked and said nothing. Despite its

abandoned air, the castle still seemed to her the most romantic place in the world.

The front door creaked open and out came a figure as cracked and neglected looking as the castle itself.

"Why, it's old Tompkins!" exclaimed the Duke.

Tompkins gave a toothless grin.

"It's myself, indeed, Your Grace. Welcome home. And is that the young mistress, Lady Sylvia? I'd recognise that golden hair anywhere."

The Duke seemed much cheered to re-encounter his old retainer. Sylvia was pleased too. She remembered Tompkins. He used to give her piggy-backs through the long corridors.

"You'll be pleased to learn cook's still here, Your Grace," went on Tompkins. "She's baked as many pies and glazed as many hams since she heard you was coming, as would feed an army."

The Duke rubbed his hands. "Well, well. I'm certainly looking forward to my supper now!"

"How many staff are there?" the Duchess asked Tompkins imperiously.

Tompkins glanced at the Duke before replying. "Not too many, Your Grace. Just myself, cook, a groom, a stable boy, a scullery maid and three housemaids."

Castle Belham had once boasted a household staff of fifty.

"But I shall need a lady's maid!" cried the Duchess.

"Plenty of time to see to that!" said the Duke quickly. "One of the housemaids can help you for now. Come along now, let's see how the old castle is keeping inside."

With a grim face, the Duchess followed her husband up the steps.

*

Sylvia threw open her window. The smell of a garden at dusk rose into the air. She turned and surveyed her room with satisfaction. The carpet was threadbare but she did not care. The canopies around the bed were moth-eaten but she did not care. There was a crack in the pier glass but she did not care. This was the room she had slept in as a child and it was full of memories. Why, there was the chair in which her mother used to sit when she came at bed-time to read to her daughter. There, above the fireplace, was the familiar portrait of her beloved mother dressed in blue satin.

A gong sounded from the entrance hall below. Throwing an embroidered Chinese shawl around her shoulders, Sylvia hurried down to supper. On the stairway she passed the painting of the Royalist, James, Duke of Belham. He looked very handsome in his plumed hat.

The Duchess was complaining about the castle as Sylvia entered the dining room.

"It needs a complete overhaul! Why, there's even mould growing on my dressing room wall."

The Duke gave a weary smile at Sylvia. He and the Duchess sat at either end of the long oak table.

Tompkins drew out a seat in the middle for Sylvia.

"It's all so ghastly!" went on the Duchess. "How am I going to invite the local families to visit? How am I going to throw parties?"

"Well – part of the plan in coming here was to get away from that sort of expense," said the Duke gently, watching as Tompkins served slices of glistening pink ham onto his plate.

"You are mad!" declared the Duchess. "How are we to find a husband for Sylvia if we cannot throw parties? Even a country Squire as husband is better than nothing. No, we must set about repairs immediately. I shall order new curtains from London tomorrow."

"But my dearest, there is no money," the Duke reminded her in a low voice, rather wishing for the moment when Tompkins were not present. The Duchess frowned at him from the other end of the table. "What, my dear?"

The Duke gave up. "I said – *there's no money.*"

"No money to at least have new curtains? No money to redecorate the rooms? Then I shall simply die!"

"You won't die when you're eating ham as good as this!" grunted the Duke, taking up his knife and fork.

"What use is ham when you have an unmarried daughter!" wailed the Duchess.

Sylvia caught Tompkin's eye. She barely suppressed a giggle while Tompkins had to cough into his white glove.

"And what about Sylvia's coming-out ball?" went on the Duchess. "When is *that* supposed to happen?"

The Duke looked uncomfortable. "I just have to sort out a few accounts, m'dear."

The Duchess went on grumbling all through dinner and Sylvia was glad when it was time to retire.

That night, she fell asleep quickly, and was soon dreaming of meadows covered in star-like flowers.

When she awoke the following morning a faint, fairy-like mist still lingered over the grass. Her heart thrilled to the song of a lark ascending the sky. She dressed hurriedly and tripped down to breakfast. Her father sat alone at table looking glum. He lit up however when he saw his daughter.

"Cook was up before dawn and baked a delicious loaf for us," he said. "There are fresh eggs too, and porridge."

"Where is Mama?" asked Sylvia as she buttered her toast. She was fond of the Duchess and called her 'Mama' even though she was not her real mother.

"She is still in bed. I told the maid to take her up some tea."

"It's such a beautiful morning," sighed Sylvia.

"It is," agreed her father. "What would you say to taking a ride?"

Sylvia's eyes widened. "There are still horses to ride here?"

"There are," nodded the Duke. "The stables are much depleted, alas, but, besides the coach horses, I still own two of the finest hunters in the county. Their sire was my old horse, Lancer."

"Then let's go!" cried Sylvia, jumping to her feet.

Her father laughed. "Aren't you eating that toast?"

"No, no. I'll have a better appetite when I come back."

Her father rose. "Well then, let's find some riding boots, shall we? I expect there's a heap of them in the tack room."

Half an hour later Sylvia and her father were riding away from the castle.

They skirted the woods and urged their horses over a fence onto open ground. Once the horses were warmed up they took to a gallop. Sylvia adored the feel of the wind in her hair.

"From the top of that hill we shall glimpse the sea," shouted the Duke over his shoulder.

The land thereabouts was flat and the hill was no more than a gentle incline. Yet it was true that from the top they were able to see the grey mass of the North Sea.

They rode down the other side of the incline to where a stream bubbled between mossy stones. Here they sat while their horses dipped their heads to drink. There was a deep silence around them, broken only by the chit-chit of a moorhen.

"Not too miserable at having to live in the country, are you?" the Duke asked his daughter after a moment.

"Oh, Papa , how can you even think that? You know that I love the countryside. It was all very well going to the Riviera every year, but I would have much preferred coming here."

"Hmmn," grunted the Duke. "Would certainly have been better for me." He sat stroking his beard for a moment. "You know, my dear, I – I have not told your step-mother and you the worst of it."

Sylvia looked at him in alarm. "What do you mean, Papa?"

The Duke looked ashamed as he told her. "I lost a great deal more than anyone knows at the casinos. On the Riviera, in Paris, in London – night after night I played and night after night I lost. I seemed to have – no luck. No luck at all. I may have to sell our London house to pay off the debts."

"Oh, Papa," murmured Sylvia. "That would be terrible. Mama is convinced that we will be able to return there one day."

The Duke sighed miserably. "Might even have to – sell Castle Belham if things get any worse."

"Sell the castle?" exclaimed Sylvia in horror.

"I'm hoping it won't come to that," said the Duke hastily. "But I simply do not have a penny to attend to all the repairs that need doing. Let alone throw you a coming-out party! Just to get us through the next year, I'm having to sell some of the paintings in the London house. I have a dealer going in there next week and he will report to me on what price he thinks he might get. But Sylvia, not a word to your step-mother, eh? I have no wish to alarm her until it is absolutely necessary. Do you promise?"

"Not a word," said Sylvia quietly.

The Duchess was at breakfast when they returned. They removed their boots and capes and went in to say good-morning.

"Oh, so you've been off enjoying yourselves," she said sourly.

"My dear, I thought after the long journey yesterday, you would like a longer rest than usual," said the Duke. "Besides, you don't care for riding."

"Riding? You've been riding? On the coach horses?"

"Of course not ," said the Duke.

"You mean you have some thoroughbreds here still?" The Duchess's eyes gleamed. "Why, we can sell them! They must be worth a great deal. I could buy curtain material and order some new carpets."

Sylvia and her father exchanged a glance.

"They're worth more in the long run as breeding stock," said the Duke.

"But we need to redecorate the castle! That's the most important thing!"

Sylvia slipped quietly from the room.

Over the next week, the Duchess kept up her litany of complaints. She seemed determined to find nothing good about the castle. She went everywhere with a notebook, and she would regale the Duke with lists of what needed to be done. The Duke looked more and more strained and Sylvia began to worry about him. Some mornings he came down unshaven to breakfast. He spent a great deal of time in his study, where he sat rolling a glass of whiskey in his hand and staring into the fire.

He never again rode out with his daughter in the morning.

Sylvia began to think of her hours riding alone as a time of escape.

She loved the castle but the atmosphere between the Duke and his wife had become oppressive. They seemed to do little but quarrel about money.

23

Galloping over the heath-land on her mare, Columbine, Sylvia could forget all about her father's gambling and her step-mother's extravagance.

Each day, she ventured farther afield. One day she even rode as far north as the mouth of the estuary. A large stone manor with square towers stood amidst wind-swept trees close to the water's edge. It looked an interesting house and Sylvia wondered who lived there. She rode down on to the road and examined the gates of the manor. FARRON TOWERS was inscribed on the pillars.

On the way back from the estuary she passed another pair of iron gates set in an archway. Over the archway was engraved the name ENDECOTT. A driveway disappeared along an avenue of elms.

Both Farron Towers and Endecott seemed to be the only houses of importance in that area to the north of Belham. The countryside around was sparsely populated. Sylvia was sure most people would call it bleak, but she loved the wild acres of heather and gorse.

To the south of Belham, the land was more undulating. There were rises and hollows where smoke rose from the chimneys of little cross-timbered cottages. Sylvia enjoyed riding here as well.

She rarely encountered another human being and yet sometimes she had the distinct feeling that she was being watched. Once she saw a horse and rider at the top of an escarpment, the rider seemingly staring her way. Another time, pausing to get her bearings in the wood that bordered the heath, she heard the cracking of twigs amidst the trees. She peered about her but saw nothing.

One grey morning a mist descended as Sylvia was riding near the estuary. She could not see a yard in front of her. She guided Columbine carefully over the rocky ground. The mist curled around horse and rider, tasting of the sea. After a while Sylvia realised that she had no idea of whether or not she was still moving in the right direction. She reined in Columbine and listened for the wash of the estuary water, which should be close to her on the right. She heard not a sound.

She was worried because she knew there was an area of quick sand near the estuary in which, it was rumoured, many had become trapped. The sun had been shining half an hour before, but now the air was chill and Sylvia wished she had brought her cape. Then she saw Columbine's ears prick up. She listened. Was something or somebody coming their way?

Suddenly a swathe of mist cleared and she gave a gasp. There ahead stood a horse and rider. The rider wore a thick muffler above which two piercing eyes seemed already fixed on Sylvia, as if they had been watching her for some time. She shivered under their cold gaze. Then the mist shifted once again and the image before her disappeared.

"Hello? Hello?" cried Sylvia.

There was no answer.

She sat and waited, too anxious to advance or retreat, until at last the mist cleared.

Whoever had appeared on the path ahead had gone.

Sylvia rode quickly home. In the past she would have mentioned such an experience to her father, but these days she had no wish to add to his concerns. After that however she never rode out without the two, fierce stable dogs as company. At least they could always lead her home if she got lost.

One day she stayed out until late afternoon. She came home via the road. The gates to the estate were now left propped open, which was just as well, as the gatekeeper was no-where to be seen. The dogs loped off well ahead of her, knowing they were now very near their bowls and baskets.

Sylvia trotted happily along between the trees. In the

soft earth of the roadway she noticed fresh hoof marks leading towards the castle. Someone else on horseback had preceded her that day. She wondered who it might be.

Outside the castle a bay mare was tethered to a ring set in the ground. The stable boy sat on the castle steps drawing in the dirt with a twig. He leapt to his feet as Sylvia rode up.

"Who is our visitor?" asked Sylvia as she slid from the saddle.

"A gentl'man," sniffed the boy. "Leastwise, by his coat. I'd not say so by his manners."

"Oh," said Sylvia. "Was he rude to you?"

"He were!" said the boy. "He just threw the reins at me and said, 'mind my horse or I'll box your ears.' What do you think of that, Lady Sylvia?"

"I think it's very unkind," agreed Sylvia. "I don't like him already!"

The boy grinned happily at this token of solidarity. He loved Sylvia and would do anything for her.

He led Columbine off to the stable while Sylvia went straight into the castle.

Tompkins met her in the hall.

"Her Grace said I was to catch you the minute you come in, as there's a visitor."

Sylvia hesitated. She would like to have changed out of her riding habit. However, if the visitor should leave before she came down, she knew the Duchess would be mortified.

"Where are they?" she asked.

"In the drawing room, Lady Sylvia," replied Tompkins.

Brushing aside the strand of hair that had come loose, she entered the drawing room.

The Duke was standing with his back to the fireplace,

regarding his wife with pleasure. The Duchess was obviously ecstatic to at last have a visitor. Her colour was high, her eyes gleamed, and she was chattering away with great animation.

"Of course, we haven't been here long," she was saying. "We plan to do a great deal to the place, as you can imagine. I've been so busy ordering things from London, I've had no time to call on my neighbours."

She broke off as she caught sight of her step-daughter.

"Oh, Sylvia," she beckoned from her seat. "You must meet Count von Brauer. So kind of him to call."

A figure rose from the depths of a wing chair that was turned away from the door through which Sylvia had entered. Two piercing eyes regarded her and for a moment she gave a start. Could this possibly be the rider she had glimpsed through the mist? The next moment she shrugged the thought away as the figure advanced and, grasping her hand, raised it warmly to his lips.

"Charmed to meet you," said the Count.

He was looking at Sylvia so intently that she blushed.

"How…do you…do?" she said.

The Count had thin eyebrows and a thin dark moustache. His nose was very fine and his lips turned down at the corners.

"Would you believe it," beamed the Duchess, "though the Count has a vast estate in Bavaria, he has come to our part of the country to look for a property to buy!"

"Do you…know this part of England well?" asked Sylvia.

The Count gave a bow. "It is an area of which I am very fond. There are a lot of mountains where I live in Bavaria, but one gets bored with mountains."

"Oh," said Sylvia, wondering how one could ever get tired of mountains. The Count still stood there regarding her, as she cast around for something else to say. "You speak…English…very well."

The Count gave another bow. "Thank you, I was educated in England. Indeed, I have spent more time here than I have in Germany. I inherited the Bavarian estate from an unmarried great-uncle on my mother's side."

"Count von Brauer has rented a house here – Endecott – while he is looking for a suitable property to buy," explained the Duchess.

"I have passed it when out riding," said Sylvia. "There is a beautiful avenue of elms leading from the gate."

"You ride a great deal," said the Count.

Sylvia drew in her breath. How did the Count know how often she went out riding?

As if reading her thoughts he gave a little shrug. "Your father told me that you are such a skilled horsewoman, he has no fear for you riding out alone every day."

"I don't know that I am so skilled. I love it, that's all," said Sylvia. She was growing uncomfortable under the Count's unblinking stare.

"You must ride over to visit me at Endecott," said the Count. "It has a splendid rose garden. The roses will soon be in bloom."

Sylvia bobbed a curtsey and stepping round the Count, went to sit beside the Duchess. The Count followed her with his eyes.

"Your daughter would make such a charming picture in my garden," he murmured.

"Wouldn't she, though!" cried the Duchess. "Not in that dreary old riding habit, but in her yellow muslin and hat – the hat she wore at Ascot – she would delight your eye."

A strange silence fell. Sylvia's eye was drawn to the Count's riding whip, which he was tapping against his boot. Tap tap tap. She wished he would stop.

The Duke seemed to suddenly bestir himself. "We must offer you some further refreshment, Count von Brauer. Yes. A glass of sherry, perhaps?"

"Thank you, Duke, but I must be on my way. I am expecting guests from London this evening."

"It is really so kind of you to call," gushed the Duchess.

The Count bowed and bade his farewell. The Duke decided not to summon Tompkins but to usher out the Count himself. He said he wished to take a look at the Count's horse.

"Well," exclaimed the Duchess as soon as the door closed behind the two men. "Who would have thought to have found such an eligible gentleman on our doorstep?"

"His lips are too thin," observed Sylvia. "And there's too much wax on his moustache."

"What? Nonsense! He has all the bearings of the aristocrat that he is. And he must be *very* rich, my dear!"

Sylvia felt obliged to remain seated while the Duchess continued to extol the virtues of the Count von Brauer. She glanced up in relief when her father at last re-entered the room. She was surprised at how cheerful he suddenly looked.

"Interesting fellow," he remarked, rubbing his hands together. "You know, I kept thinking I'd seen his face before! Turns out he used to spend his summers on the Riviera."

The Duchess frowned. "And frequented the casinos, no doubt?" The Duke gave a cough. "Yes – as a matter of fact."

"Well, no doubt he could afford it!" sniffed the Duchess. "And no doubt he wasn't so foolish as to lose his entire fortune at the tables!"

The Duke looked a little embarrassed. "Can't say how

he fared, m'dear. Never played a game with him, you understand. Must have noted him at some point, though. An arresting visage, wouldn't you say?"

"Indeed," said the Duchess, mollified for a moment only. "I do hope we see him again soon."

"As a matter of fact," said the Duke, "he's, er – invited me over to Endecott to join him and his guests this evening."

The Duchess stiffened. "Invited – *you* – on your own?"

"Yes. The Count apologises that it is a gentlemen only evening, but said he hopes to invite the ladies of Belham another time."

"And what exactly will take place at this gentlemen only evening?" asked the Duchess.

Sylvia held her breath. She knew what her step-mother was thinking.

"Oh," said the Duke nonchalantly, "his guests are all members of his London club so – a lot of shop talk. Business, politics, hunting – that sort of thing."

The Duchess tightened her lips. "No doubt 'that sort of thing' will involve a game or two of cards?"

The Duke had turned, whistling, to the fire. "What, my dear? Cards? Oh, it's possible, no doubt. I shan't play myself, of course."

Sylvia and the Duchess exchanged a glance.

There was one subject on which they were both perfectly agreed.

The Duke could no more refuse to play a game of cards than he could refuse to breathe.

Yet they were helpless. The Duke had already accepted the Count's invitation. It would be extremely discourteous to change the arrangement.

All they could do this evening was hope!

CHAPTER THREE

An owl was hooting outside Sylvia's window. *Tooowhit tooowhoooo.* The sound startled her awake in her armchair by the fire. As she straightened up, the book she had been reading slipped from her lap and fell heavily to the floor. She bent to retrieve it. What was the title? Oh yes…'The Folklore of Norfolk.' She had barely read the preface before she had dozed off.

She wondered how long she had been asleep. She felt rather stiff. Cold too, despite the thick shawl over her night-dress. She glanced at the hearth and saw that the fire was out.

Toooowhit tooowhooo. One rarely heard owls in London and the sound delighted her. Then came another muffled sound, the old clock along the corridor striking the hour. She opened her bedroom door to hear more keenly. Ting ting ting ting – four o'clock! She had been asleep in her armchair since just after midnight!

Her father had set off at seven for his evening at Count von Brauer's house, Endecott. Sylvia had been unable to sleep, waiting for his return. At midnight she had got out of bed, stoked the fire and settled down in her armchair with a book. That was the last thing she remembered.

Her father must be back by now. She had been too deeply asleep to hear his horse, that was all.

She crossed to the bed, threw her shawl across it, and

slipped gratefully beneath the covers. Teeth beginning to chatter, she sought the warming pan that must be lurking at the foot of the mattress. Her feet finally encountered the copper but quickly withdrew. The pan was quite cold.

She curled up on her side and closed her eyes. The owl had stopped hooting. She imagined a rush of wing beyond her window…the squeal of a field-mouse in the orchard…a white-ruffed shape bearing its spoil aloft…and pitied for a moment the tiny creatures that ended the night as prey. Her mind drifted on and she saw the owl rise higher, higher, under the glitter of a distant star…Arcturus the Pathfinder.

Her eyes flew open as she heard the trot of a horse's hooves on the road.

She threw back the bedclothes and ran to the window.

Below, a horse and rider slowly approached the castle. She recognised her father's bent and weary head. Swiftly taking up her shawl, she opened her bedroom door and tip-toed along the corridor. She passed the Duchess' bedchamber and paused for an instant. Yes, she could hear a light snore that indicated her step-mother was asleep. If she could reach the front door before her father pulled the bell, no-one would know he had returned so late. She could not explain to herself why her heart was full of foreboding.

She reached the main staircase and ran lightly down the steps. She tugged open the main door and caught her father dismounting. He stood for a moment with the reins in his hand, staring at the ground. Without a thought for herself, scantily clad on this chill April night, Sylvia hurried down the steps to his side.

Her father looked up in surprise. "M'dear." His face looked so grey, so pinched with cold, that she was alarmed. Something was wrong!

"Papa…come in quickly…just tether up Belami…I'll get him stabled later."

The Duke did as he was told, like a child. He followed Sylvia back into the castle. She was uncertain of where to take him at this hour. Where would be warm? She thought of the great stove in the kitchen and decided to take him there. He trotted meekly at her side.

The stove was still warm and Sylvia pulled a chair up close for her father. She drew up a chair for herself opposite. She knew cook would be up soon to start the baking for the day. She would ask her to prepare her father something warm. Meanwhile she must find out why he looked so stunned.

She leaned forward and rubbed his hands, almost blue with cold, between her own. She noticed that his beard smelled of whiskey and tobacco.

"Papa?"

His eyes, watery and somehow fearful, met hers. "M'dear?"

"You are…home so late. It will soon be dawn."

"Will it, m'dear? I – hadn't noticed."

"What kept you at Endecott till this hour?"

The Duke blinked at her. Suddenly his eyes filled with tears and he gave a moan.

"Oh, we are undone. Completely undone."

Sylvia's heart sank. Although she half guessed the answer, still she heard herself asking the question. "What…has happened, Papa?"

"I was – on a run of luck, m'dear. The others had dropped out – only the Count and myself left – and I had a good hand – I could have sworn – no-one could have had a better – and yet – I lost. I lost."

Sylvia felt that her heart was encased in ice. "How much, Papa?"

Her father could not meet her gaze. "A great deal – yes, a great deal. At least – ten thousand pounds."

Ten thousand pounds! Sylvia could not speak. She sat back and stared at the floor. Ten thousand pounds. How would her father ever repay the Count?

She looked up as she heard a strangled sound. Her father's chest heaved as he tried to repress a sob. A wave of pity flooded through her. Her father looked so tired and ill. She must get him to bed before the Duchess rose. That would at least spare her father himself from having to tell his wife the bad news. She, Sylvia, would tell her step-mother everything at breakfast.

She gently took her father's arm and helped him from the chair. He seemed to have lost all sense of strength and purpose. She led him from the kitchen and up the servants' staircase to his room. She helped him off with his boots and then he fell fully clothed into bed. He began snoring almost immediately. Sylvia drew the cover over him and crept from the room.

She had no idea of what would happen now to her family and to Castle Belham.

*

The Duchess raised her arms and Polly nervously dropped the silk dress over her mistress's head. Polly was all fingers. She had never dreamed that she would be one day elevated from humble housemaid to ladies' maid, and she was not sure she liked it. She didn't like handling all these expensive things, silk and satin and voile, goldplated hairbrushes and delicate tortoiseshell combs. Suppose she tore something or broke something? The Duchess was so finicky too and always scolding her for no reason. She'd have much preferred to be back at her old duties, where she at least had company.

"Now hand me my stockings, Polly," ordered the Duchess.

Polly glanced round anxiously. Where had the laundry

maid put the clean stockings this morning? Were they there, in that blue basket? She took out a soft, white pair and handed them to the Duchess, who sat on the bed. At least her mistress didn't expect Polly to pull up her stockings for her! The Duchess drew one half way up her leg and then gave a cry.

"Oh, Polly, there's a hole in this! Did you take it from that basket? Everything in there is to go for repair. My clean stockings are in the chest of drawers."

Sullenly, Polly marched over to the rosewood chest of drawers and, opening the top drawer, took out an embroidered stocking bag.

There was a knock at the bedroom door.

"Mama?"

"Is that you, Sylvia? Come in, do."

Sylvia entered. She looked pale and there were circles under her eyes. She had not been able to sleep at all since her father's return in the early hours of the morning.

"Sylvia, you look perfectly dreadful. Are you sick or something? Polly, that pair will do – the grey silk pair, thank you."

Sylvia sat on the end of her stepmother's bed. "I'd like to…talk to you," she said. "In private."

The Duchess regarded Sylvia sharply and then turned to Polly. "Polly, you may go for the moment. I'll finish dressing myself."

Polly bobbed a curtsey and, with an almost baleful look at Sylvia, left the room.

"Now, what is troubling you?" asked the Duchess.

In a low voice Sylvia told the Duchess about the Duke's night at Endecott. She had barely finished speaking when the Duchess leapt to her feet with her hands to her face.

"Oh, this is a disaster! How could he! How could he! We are ruined beyond all hope of rescue. How will we ever find you a husband?"

"I assure you, that is not my main concern at the moment," said Sylvia. "I am worried about Papa. He is not himself."

"Not himself?" The Duchess looked flushed and angry. "Oh, he's himself all right. Losing at cards is a favourite pastime of his. Why did I ever let him go to Endecott?"

"Why did the Count ever invite him?" mused Sylvia. It was a question that had troubled her all morning.

"Oh, don't you go blaming it all on the Count," cried the Duchess. "He is above reproach. He did not force your father to play, I'll be bound."

"He may have been well aware that he didn't have to," countered Sylvia. "He may have heard the gossip at the casinos about the Duke of Belham's habit."

"I won't hear such nonsense! All the man did was issue an innocent invitation. No, no. It's your father's fault. To think that when I married him I was considered a lucky young woman!"

Sylvia said nothing. The Duchess had not been so young when she married the Duke and coming as she did from impoverished landed gentry, there had been no reason in the world *not* to think her lucky. She had certainly enjoyed spending her new husband's money.

The Duchess stood wringing her hands. "Ten thousand pounds! We'll have to sell the London house."

Sylvia lowered her eyes. Obviously her father had not told the Duchess that it was already on the cards, long before his most recent and ignominious loss at cards.

"What are we going to do, what are we going to do?" wailed the Duchess. "I can't – I simply can't – be *poor*." Suddenly she wheeled on Sylvia. "You must appeal to his good nature."

"Whose?" asked Sylvia, bewildered.

"Why, Count von Brauer's!" said the Duchess impatiently. "He obviously admired you. He said you would make a pretty picture in his garden."

"I think he might admire me ten thousand pounds less now," observed Sylvia dryly.

"Nonsense, nonsense!" cried the Duchess. "You must ask him to defer the repayment. Use your charms. Buy some time."

Sylvia thought dully that buying time would buy them nothing. The debt would still have to be paid eventually. However she said that she would think about speaking to the Count herself when the moment came.

The moment came sooner than she expected.

She and the Duchess were sitting at breakfast – neither of them eating much beyond a slice of toast – when Tompkins entered the dining room to tell them that Count von Brauer had called and awaited the Duke in the library.

The Duchess, flurried, dropped her napkin. "Oh. He's here – already. Summon the Duke, Tompkins."

Tompkins glanced at Sylvia before replying, "the Duke is still asleep, my lady. I opened his curtains at nine o'clock, but seeing him dead to the world I drew them again. I believe he had a very late night. His horse was tethered outside the door instead of in the stable."

Sylvia realised she had forgotten all about poor Belami.

"Still asleep?" repeated the Duchess. "Well, you must wake him."

Sylvia recalled the confused state of her father the night before. Wishing to spare him further scenes of humiliation for now, she made up her mind.

"Tell the Count that I will speak to him," she said.

The Duchess clasped her hands together. "You will?

Oh, that is marvellous!"

Sylvia sighed. She did not believe for an instant that the Count's admiration for her would over-ride his interest in calling in the debt.

"I must run and put on a dress," said the Duchess, who was still in her morning gown. "Tompkins, will you send me up Polly?"

Tompkins hesitated. "I'm afraid, Your Grace, that Polly seems to have run off.'

"Run off?" echoed the Duchess. "Why on earth! Oh, drat the girl. I'll have to train up one of the others. Send me Jeannie."

Tompkins bowed and left the room.

"I had better go and confront the Count," said Sylvia, rising.

"One moment!' The Duchess hurried over to her. That strand of hair is too loose – see – let me tuck it up. And your cheeks – far too pale. I'll give them a pinch."

Sylvia submitted to her step-mother's ministrations without a word. Soon there was a spot of red on each cheek and her hair, that she had not yet styled, was arranged neatly behind her ears. She turned and walked to the door.

"Do your best," urged the Duchess, sinking back down into her chair.

Sylvia walked quietly along the corridor to the library. She did not knock but pushed open the door and entered. The Count was standing with his back to her, examining the books arrayed on a shelf in one of the bookcases. He turned when he heard her step. His eye ran almost insolently over her figure and she suddenly wished she were wearing something with a higher neckline.

"Lady Sylvia," he exclaimed.

Sylvia swallowed and held out her hand. The Count took it and raised it lingeringly to his lips.

"Would you…care for some tea?" asked Sylvia, withdrawing her hand in as polite a manner as she could.

"Thank you, no," replied the Count. "I was hoping to speak to the Duke."

"My father is…still resting." Sylvia felt her voice begin to tremble. "I do not want to disturb him. I believe he had…a most distressing time last night."

"Well, that's his version," shrugged the Count.

Sylvia was shocked. "His *version*? Are you saying…he distorted the facts?"

The Count raised his hand and started to twirl his moustache between thumb and forefinger. "If I remember correctly – the Duke ate a pound of wild salmon and half a lobster. Consumed half a bottle of good Scotch. Smoked four or five excellent cigars. And held a damn good brace of cards for most of the game. Does that sound like a distressing evening to you?"

"No doubt he *was* enjoying himself at first," said Sylvia. "But all that changed when…"

"When his luck ran out? The Count shrugged. "My dear young lady, the Duke is a practised hand at the card table. He knows the score."

"He plays until he loses it all!" cried Sylvia. "That is his pattern. Everybody knows that."

"Everybody?"

"Yes. Everybody who frequents the casinos, the clubs. My father's weakness is legendary. We have kept him away from the casinos recently, but now…"

Here Sylvia had to break off for fear that she would begin to sob.

"But now he owes me a considerable sum of money," ended the Count with a cool smile.

"Yes," whispered Sylvia, lowering her eyes.

"And you want me to show a little mercy, do you?"

Sylvia gave a brief nod. She could not bear to speak or beg in any way. She sensed that the Count was enjoying his position of power.

"Look at me," she heard him say. Slowly she raised her eyes. The Count's gaze was cold and calculating as he spoke. "Do I look like the kind of man who would choose to wave away a ten thousand pound debt?"

"N...no," replied Sylvia. "But that is not what I was going to ask..."

"You," snarled the Count, "are in no position to *ask* for anything."

Sylvia was stung for a moment but she took a deep breath and went on. "I only wanted to...to plead that you...do not call the debt in all at once. It would cripple my father."

The Count gave a satisfied nod. "Yes. I had rather suspected that."

Sylvia stared at him. "Then why...why did you invite my father to Endecott...why did you let him play, if you knew that he was already in trouble?"

"I had my reasons," said the Count with an insinuating smile.

Sylvia sank down onto a sofa. "I do not...understand."

The Count stood above her, gazing down. "Perhaps I can strike a bargain with the Duke."

Sylvia looked up quickly. "And not call in the debt immediately?"

"I mean not call *it in at all*."

Sylvia knew better than to think the Count intended an altruistic act.

"What would you hope for...in return?" she asked slowly.

"Oh, that is simple to answer," said the Count. "*You.*"

Sylvia recoiled in dismay. "M…me?"

"Yes," said the Count.

"Y…you mean…be your mistress?"

"Oh, come, come," laughed the Count. "Surely you do not think so ill of me as that?" He took up his whip, which lay across a small table, and stood stroking its length thoughtfully. "Strange as it may seem, I am proposing marriage. You have no dowry to speak of but – you, er – please my eye. And you are spirited. I like to tame – spirited young women."

Sylvia rose to her feet in consternation. "Really, Count. That is…that is hardly a recommendation."

With a sudden move the Count pressed the point of the whip against Sylvia's throat.

"I do not need a recommendation," he hissed. "You have only to consider your father's position. The sums are simple. If you do not accept me, he is utterly ruined."

He gave her a quick, icy smile and stepped away as the voice of the Duchess was heard in the corridor. "Sylvia, Sylvia – I don't know what to do with your father. He's insisting on getting out of bed, but I fear he is not well."

The Count turned to the door as the Duchess came hurrying through. She stopped short when she saw him.

"Oh, Count von Brauer! I thought perhaps you had gone."

The Count bowed. "As you can see, I am still a captive, Duchess."

The Duchess's eyes flew anxiously from the Duke to Sylvia. "Have you – can we – resolve the problem?" She waited a moment, and then when there was no answer began to wring her hands. "Sylvia – Count von Brauer?"

The Count gently tapped his whip against his thigh. "If by problem you mean this matter of the debt, why yes, I

41

believe we have found a way to resolve it."

The Duchess brightened. "Yes?"

The Count inclined his head. "Perhaps you should ask your step-daughter what the choices are."

The Duchess wheeled on Sylvia expectantly. "Well, my dear?"

Sylvia slowly crossed to the window and looked out at the green lawn, across which strolled two white geese. She wondered dully where they had come from.

"WELL?" The Duchess was impatient.

"Count con Brauer has suggested," said Sylvia quietly, "that he will cancel the debt on condition that I agree to be his wife."

The Duchess reeled back, her hands pressed to her bosom. "His *wife*? He has asked you to marry him?"

"Yes."

"I would also insist," said the Count quickly, "that Sylvia and I take up residence in Castle Belham immediately we were married. I've taken quite a fancy to the place and look forward to spending money on improvements."

"Oh," said the Duchess weakly.

"I would encourage you and the Duke to return to London until the works are completed," went on the Count, his eye on the Duchess.

The Duchess fell into an armchair. She seemed to be gasping for air. "This is too much – too much. All our difficulties solved – with one blow!"

Sylvia turned with a gasp. "Mama! You mean…you *agree?*"

"Dear child," cried the Duchess. "Look at the advantages! A prestigious marriage – a debt cancelled – the castle restored to its former glory! And I can return to London. Oh, the Count is most generous, indeed he is. Why, here is the Duke. He will surely be delighted."

The Duke had entered slowly on the arm of Tompkins. Sylvia caught her breath when she saw her father. His hair was dishevelled, he was unshaven, his skin was a grey colour and his shirt was unbuttoned at the neck. When he saw the Count, he drew away from Tompkins and advanced unsteadily.

"You need not think, sir, that I intended to hide in my chamber, while you were here. My servant did not wake me this morning – that is all. Believe me, sir, I am a man who always honours his debts."

"Of which there are many, I believe," observed the Count coolly.

"What? Many? Why, sir, that's of little consequence I – will pay them all, sir, even if I have to sell everything I own."

"He is not asking for that," said Sylvia with sudden bitterness. "All he is asking is that you…sell your daughter."

Count von Brauer glanced at Sylvia, amused. Meanwhile the Duke appeared bewildered.

"Sell – my daughter?"

"Oh, that's just Sylvia having a little fun," cried the Duchess quickly. She rose and bustled over to her husband. "Only think, my dear. The Count has asked for Sylvia's hand in marriage. Far from expecting a dowry he has offered to pay all the repairs to the castle. We are saved."

"S – saved?" The Duke looked slowly round the room. "Saved?"

The Count turned to Sylvia with a triumphant gleam in his eye. "Well, Lady Sylvia. It seems that my suit meets with some favour. All it needs now is your own consent."

Sylvia shuddered under his gaze. Her eye fell on the whip which he held close to his side. No, it was impossible, she could not wed this man. A fleeting image crossed her

43

mind…the garden at Lady Lambourne's…a masked man kneeling before her, his strong hand around her ankle as he slipped a satin shoe onto her foot…his gentle voice. And the stars! The wonderful, glittering stars that night.

How, after having encountered a man like that, could she ever marry this odious, leering Count von Brauer.

"I…cannot!" she gasped. "I…cannot."

She began to back towards the door, her eyes haunted.

The Duchess giggled nervously. "She is overcome, that is all. Don't you worry, Count von Brauer. All she needs is a little time and then she will favour you."

Reaching the door, Sylvia turned and stumbled through. Her step-mother's voice echoed in her ears as she ran.

"All she needs is a little time."

All the time in the world could not bring her to favour the Count!

*

The next few days were a torture for Sylvia. Her step-mother seized every opportunity to press the case for marrying the Count. Sylvia felt trapped. The weather was terrible, rain teeming down from morning to night, so there was no chance of riding out on Columbine. If she stayed in her room, the Duchess would seek her out, crying and cajoling. The Duke said very little. He seemed in a daze half the time and Sylvia had no desire to punish his mind any further.

When the Duchess urged him to entreat Sylvia to accept the Count, he shook his head stubbornly. "No, no. The child must choose for herself," he said. In the end the Duchess gave up raging at her husband and sent for Sylvia's sisters.

Edith and Charlotte arrived the very next day. They lost no time in adding their voices to the argument.

"Just consider," said Edith. "What is your position if you don't accept? Who else will marry you?"

"I don't care if no-one else marries me, I just don't want to marry *him*," replied Sylvia.

"You were always too finicky for your own good," sniffed Charlotte. "But if you don't marry, who is to keep you? Father and mother? Why, if things go on as they are, they will end up in the poor house."

"They won't!" cried Sylvia. "I would never let that happen. I would work."

"Work!" exclaimed her sisters in horror. "A lady cannot possibly *work*!"

"Times are changing," said Sylvia. "There are female teachers and nurses. Look at Florence Nightingale."

"But you're a *Belham*!" howled her sisters.

"Belham or not, I would sooner be a chimney sweep than see Papa and Mama go without. And anyway, surely you could help them? Surely your husbands would help them out?"

Edith and Charlotte looked at each other.

"They are reluctant to intervene, they have their own families to think of, both of us are expectant mothers and besides, there is now a perfectly good alternative."

Sylvia turned away, her hands over her ears. She was in despair but determined not to succumb to such pressure.

After supper everyone retired early. Sylvia went to bed and lay in the dark, unable to sleep.

'I'll count stars in my head,' she thought idly. 'That's far better than sheep.'

At that moment a terrible scream rent the air. It came from the Duke's room, just below Sylvia's, and she started up in terror. Without waiting to throw on a robe, she flew out of the room and along the corridor. Out of the corner of her eye she saw doors opening and sleepy heads peering out.

"What's going on?" called Edith as she passed.

"It's Papa," shouted Sylvia.

She ran on, down the stairs, along the corridor. The Duchess met her at the door to the Duke's room, her face white with terror.

"I c..came in to say g..good-night and f..found him on the floor," she stammered. "He won't say a word, he's just staring into space. T..Tompkins has sent for the d..doctor."

Sylvia raced in to the Duke. The Duchess had been unable to lift him onto the bed, so he sat propped against a chest of drawers. His skin had a bluish tinge to it and he was barely breathing.

Sylvia found herself praying. 'Please, God, don't take Papa away from me!'

Edith and Charlotte appeared. With her sisters' aid Sylvia was able to manoeuvre her father onto the bed and lay him down. She tenderly drew the quilt over him and then they waited.

Two hours later the doctor turned away from the bed where the Duke lay and regarded the three sisters and their step-mother gravely.

"A nervous collapse," he said. "I believe he has been under a great deal of mental stress recently. It has taken its toll. His heart is weak. He needs rest and *no more worry*."

Edith and Charlotte fixed angry eyes on Sylvia.

"You see," said Edith. "You see! If you had accepted the Count three days ago, this wouldn't have happened. Papa could have stopped worrying about money!"

Sylvia burst into tears.

"Hush, now, hush," said the Duchess. "There's no use scolding about the past. It's the future that is the problem."

"Indeed it is," nodded the doctor, glancing at Sylvia. "His mind is not strong at the moment. He cannot take much anxiety."

Edith, Charlotte and the Duchess all pursed their lips. Sylvia looked from one to the other wildly. Then she looked at her father, lying so deathly still and pale in the bed. She alone had the power to remove all care from his shoulders. She alone could ensure that his health and strength returned.

With this knowledge, her fate was sealed.

She hung her head and spoke in a voice so low that the Duchess had to strain to hear.

"You may tell the Count that I accept, Mama. Tell him that I agree to be his wife."

As the Duchess clapped her hands and the two sisters hugged each other for joy, Sylvia slipped quietly and disconsolately from the room.

CHAPTER FOUR

A pale sun struggled to shine as Sylvia rode up the avenue that led to Castle Belham. There was barely a sound. Just the drip of rain from wet leaves, or the odd sucking noise as her horse drew a hoof up from the muddy ground.

That morning, after what had seemed like weeks of bad weather, the skies had finally cleared. This had decided Sylvia to accompany her sisters' coach as far as the gates of the estate. She said good-bye to them there. Now that they had, as they thought, achieved their purpose, now that Sylvia was going to marry 'that fine looking fellow, the Count,' Edith and Charlotte were in magnanimous mood. They chatted to her merrily and begged to be matrons of honour.

"You must come up to London to choose your trousseau," urged Edith.

"And we insist that you are god-mother to our babies!" cried Charlotte. "Won't the next year be great fun!"

"It's a pity you're not going to have a coming-out, of course," sighed Edith.

"Now, now, getting married is coming-out enough!" said Charlotte, with a warning glance at Edith.

They could not but notice that Sylvia was quiet and downcast and it piqued their consciences a little. They tried to reassure her. After all, *they* had not married for love. They had married for security and look how well it had turned out. Admittedly Edith was happier when her husband was abroad on diplomatic business and Charlotte never minded when her husband spent the night at his club but nothing was ever *perfect*.

Sylvia listened in silence.

The last three days had passed in a dull haze. The Count was informed of her decision, but Sylvia would not see him for the present. The Duchess made her excuses, saying that Sylvia was distraught at her father's illness and in no mood for company. The Count bowed and said he would await a summons from his fiancée, but that he was anxious for the marriage to take place as soon as possible. The Duchess demurred – she had visions of a splendid, county wedding and that required time to plan.

Eventually a compromise of the end of June was agreed. This set the Duchess in excited motion. She sent for her own wedding dress from London, where it lay under tissue in a trunk. It was a beautiful dress of white beaded satin and she was sure it could be altered to a more fashionable style for Sylvia. She started lists – gifts and guests and gourmet food.

Try as she or the sisters might, however, they could not interest Sylvia in the details. She stared listlessly at materials for a veil, patterns for altering the dress, ideas for the wedding breakfast. Let the Duchess decide, she said. She did not care.

She tried harder with her father. When the Duke took her hand as she sat at his bedside and asked if she were happy she nodded brightly.

"Oh, yes, Papa, wonderfully."

"Good, good," said the Duke, closing his eyes. "He's a rich fellow, anyway. You'll want for nothing."

As her father drifted into sleep, Sylvia gazed at his face. The lines of worry that had creased his brow were smoothing out, colour was returning to his cheeks.

Her sacrifice was not in vain.

This was the thought that comforted her as she waved off her sisters and turned her horse for home.

She broke from the trees. The castle was now visible, its spires seeming to pierce the sky. She reined in Columbine and sat for a moment, savouring the air, which almost tasted of damp grass.

She tried to imagine herself living at Castle Belham with the Count. No doubt they would occupy the large bedroom that had once been her parents' room, when her own mother was alive.

The idea made her tremble.

The castle that she loved so much suddenly looked empty, friendless.

She glanced up at the sky. Tompkins had said that the break in the weather was temporary. Storms were forecast for later. But the sky, though grey, was smooth as slate. There was no sign of ominous dark clouds.

On an impulse Sylvia turned her horse to the left and rode towards the open fields. No-one would be seeking her out this morning. She could ride free until lunch time.

Her spirits lifted as Columbine cleared the low bushes that bordered the estate to the west and galloped on towards the heath. Columbine's hooves threw up clods of damp turf. Sylvia laughed aloud as her hair streamed behind her.

She turned to the east and made for the estuary.

After weeks of virtual imprisonment in the castle, after all the unhappy dramas of the last few days, Sylvia felt carefree again. She meant to return to the castle for lunch but she lost track of time. She felt neither hunger nor fatigue and Columbine seemed as high spirited as herself.

She rode to the mouth of the estuary and the house with its stone towers that stood there on the promontory. The garden of this house sloped steeply down to the water's edge. It seemed an ideal spot.

As she sat there she saw a coach drive out from the stable yard. The coach drew up outside the entrance to the house. Two figures emerged from the house, a man and a woman, both wrapped in cloaks. They climbed into the coach and it set off along the road to the west. It was probably going to the town of Sheringham, along the coast.

The sight of the cloaks made Sylvia realise that the wind had changed. It had developed a keen, cold edge to it. She shivered. It was surely time to return.

She rode along the estuary. The wind sent waves scudding along its surface. She pulled up the hood of her cape and bent her head against the stinging air.

Suddenly Columbine reared to a halt. Sylvia grasped at his mane as she was thrown forward. Her hood fell back as she righted herself in the saddle and looked ahead.

Count von Brauer sat astride his large bay horse, blocking Sylvia's way forward.

"I called at Castle Belham," said the Count. "They have been most anxious about you since you did not appear for lunch. I said that I would ride out and find you."

"And so you have," said Sylvia through gritted teeth.

"Yes," replied the Count. "And so far from home!"

Sylvia narrowed her eyes. "You knew I might be on this road. You have…waylaid me here before."

"Waylaid?"

"There was a mist. It cleared a little and you were sitting there on that horse. Why did you not make yourself known? Why did you disappear?"

The Count hesitated for a moment and then shrugged. "Let us say I was too shy to introduce myself."

"Shy!" exclaimed Sylvia.

"Ah!" sighed the Count. "You persist in holding an unfavourable opinion of me. You cannot imagine that an admirer, who had been following you for some time should find himself unable to approach the woman he adored." He looked at her with an almost mocking air and then continued. "Were you frightened?"

"Yes," said Sylvia. "I was. But I think it pleases you to know that. I think you like frightening women."

The Count's eyes narrowed. "That is an accusation you may make only when you know me better. And you will – know me better."

Sylvia's eye moved unwillingly to the whip that the Count held, resting lightly across the neck of his horse. The Count followed her gaze and gave a cold smile. "You guess that – I will discipline without hesitation – those creatures that are under my charge."

Her heart beginning to pound, Sylvia spoke in a low voice. "I wish to go home now."

"To Castle Belham? Oh, but they are not expecting you there. The Duke and Duchess have agreed to drive to my house at Endecott for supper."

"My father…is not well enough to visit anyone," cried Sylvia in dismay.

"Did you see him this morning?" asked the Count quickly.

"N..no," admitted Sylvia.

"He is remarkably improved. He said he was looking forward to dining with us."

"*Us*?"

"I said I would take you straight to Endecott when I found you."

Sylvia felt at that moment as if she could not breathe. "How could they be sure…you would find me?"

For a second only, the Count faltered. "Why I said I

knew for certain – which way you had gone. Your tracks in the mud – "

Sylvia shrank into her cloak. She had no desire to ride on with the Count to his house at Endecott. As if reading her thoughts, the Count tried to speak in a gentler tone.

"Look about you. Rain is on its way and Endecott is much closer than Belham."

Sylvia gazed around. It was indeed true that black clouds were moving swiftly in from the sea, whipped on by the wind.

Leaning quickly forward, the Count took hold of Columbine's rein.

"Come," he said. "I will lead you on. Your parents will have left Belham by the time *you* arrive there. Why cause them a moment's more worry than is necessary?"

Cold and hungry now and convinced at last of his argument, Sylvia allowed herself to be led towards Endecott and its avenue of elms.

*

The clouds opened before they reached the house. The stable boy ran forward to take their mounts, while the Count ushered Sylvia into the dark entrance hall of Endecott. The Count then went to the end of the hallway to call for his valet.

A maid came forward from the shadows to take Sylvia's cape. Sylvia eyes widened when she saw who it was.

"Polly!"

"That's right."

"Why did you…run off without a word?"

"I suppose I can go where I like without permission, can't I?" scowled Polly. "I liked the look of the Count, so I thought I'd ask him for work. I don't have to find no stockings or do up buttons *here*."

Sylvia said nothing more as the Count returned.

"Show my – fiancée – to the red room, there's a good girl, Polly. She can freshen up there," said the Count.

Polly made a face when she heard Sylvia referred to as 'fiancée'. She flounced up the stairs ahead of Sylvia and led her into a room whose walls were painted a deep blood red. A large canopied bed took up most of the space. Sylvia noticed that a huge fire was set in the grate.

"Perhaps you will light the fire, Polly?"

"I'm not *your* maid, you know, miss," sniffed Polly.

Sylvia turned away. Polly spoke out of turn but Sylvia was not sure that the Count would listen to complaints about her. Sylvia had a suspicion that he might rather enjoy his fiancée's discomfort.

She dropped onto the stool before the dressing table and stared at herself. Being engaged did not suit her at all, she thought wryly. She looked wan and her eyes had none of their one time sparkle.

She took up a brush that lay on the dressing table and began to brush the damp hair back from her forehead. After a moment her hand dropped to her side. She bowed her head before her listless image and wept silently.

She was roused by the sound of hail clattering at the window. A blinding white flash lit up the room and simultaneously lit up her startled, white face in the mirror. A moment later came the deep, brutish growl of thunder.

In the glass she saw the door behind her open and Polly leered in.

"Your *fiancé* says you're to come down for some tea."

"I'd rather wait here until my parents arrive," said Sylvia quietly.

"What makes you think they're coming *here*?" asked Polly with genuine surprise.

"Why, the…the Count said they were expected."

"First I've heard of it," snorted Polly.

"He may well not have informed you. Perhaps he informed the cook."

Polly snorted again. "*I'm* the cook."

"Y..you are?"

"There's only me, the valet, and the stable boy. And a woman who comes to clean but she's under *my* instructions," said Polly haughtily.

Sylvia felt sick with apprehension. If her parents were not coming to Endecott tonight, then the Count had lied to her. The question was, why?

"Anyway, you're to come down," said Polly, bored now with the situation.

Almost in a daze, Sylvia rose and followed Polly down to the drawing room.

The Count was lolling in a large wing chair before the fire. He did not rise when Sylvia entered but merely gestured at her to sit opposite him. She sat, desiring to wait until Polly had left the room before she spoke. Polly seemed to dawdle over the tea things, which stood ready on an occasional table. She even started to hum a tune. The Count watched Sylvia with an amused expression.

At last Polly brought over the tea and poured out each cup. She then turned her nose into the air and left the room. No sooner had the door closed behind her than Sylvia put down her cup and confronted her fiancé.

"Why did you mislead me, Sir?"

"Mislead you?"

"Oh, come. You know what I am talking about. You said my parents were invited here tonight."

The Count lowered his gaze mockingly. "I did. I'm a rogue. I admit it."

Sylvia stared. "You…admit it?"

"How else was I going to have you to myself? For days you have refused to see me. It is more than a full-blooded man can bear."

Sylvia leapt to her feet, knocking her cup of tea from the little table before her.

"How…how dare you! My parents will be so anxious…not knowing where I am".

The Count gave a nonchalant wave of his hand. "Oh, they'll know where you are soon enough. I'll send the stable boy to Castle Belham with a message. Poor fellow. He will have to stay there overnight if the storm does not abate."

The implication of this struck Sylvia cruelly. If the stable boy had to stay at Castle Belham because of the storm, that same fact meant *she* would have to stay at Endecott!

"I must go, I must go home now!" said Sylvia in great agitation.

"Don't be a fool," said the Count. "Listen to the wind. Look out of the window. See how the trees are thrashing, see how the rain is falling. You would be in grave danger if you set out now. The boy is a hardy young fellow, but *you* – you cannot risk the journey. And your parents would not thank me if I permitted it."

Slowly Sylvia sank back into her seat. She stared at the ground, feeling like a creature caught in a trap. It was true that she would be in grave danger if she tried to ride home. But would she be in even graver danger if she remained here with the Count?

The Count is your fiancé, she reminded herself. Why should he wish you harm? She lifted her eyes to his. He was sprawled in his chair, at great ease, twirling his moustache between thumb and forefinger as he watched her. She wondered dully how often in the years ahead she would watch him do this.

She begged leave to return to her room until supper. The Count acquiesced, content that she appeared to have accepted her temporary confinement at his house. As she mounted the stairs she was aware of Polly regarding her through an open door at the end of the corridor.

She remained in the red room for the next couple of hours, curled up on a chaise longue. She had taken the quilt from the bed to keep herself warm. She listened hopefully for a lessening of the storm. To no avail. The wind seemed to rise higher and higher until it was screeching at the casement. Rain teemed, drawing a thick grey curtain between the window and the outside world.

She wondered as she waited there why the Count had so few staff. Surely he could afford to maintain a larger household?

She knew so little about him and yet she was about to yoke herself to him for the rest of her life.

Yet what choice had she? It was either that, or see her father's health further destroyed.

She was most uneasy when she joined the Count for supper. The table was laid for two in a gloomy dining room. Candles flickered in tall candlesticks and there were two bottles of wine open on a sideboard.

Polly served, with a curious sneer on her face. Sylvia ignored her. She was surprised to find that she was hungry. The meal of lamb shank and red cabbage was better than she expected. She declined to drink any wine. The Count however finished glass after glass.

He spoke at great length of his estates in Bavaria, his aristocratic friends, his visits to hunting lodges with the Prince of Wales. Sylvia kept glancing at the clock on the mantelpiece. The hand crept on towards nine and still the storm raged.

The Count suggested they repair to the drawing room

for coffee. Sylvia noted with apprehension that he staggered for a moment at the door.

In the drawing room he insisted Sylvia sit on the sofa beside him. He sat with his arm across the back of the sofa behind Sylvia. She was aware of his hand brushing against her shoulder. With sinking heart Sylvia saw that the clock in this room now said half past ten.

She knew she must bow to the inevitable and remain at Endecott for the night. She therefore broached the subject of the fire in her room with the Count. Would he please order Polly to light it?

"What, is my little chicken cold then?" The Count's words were slurred.

At this moment Polly came in with the coffee. Sylvia glanced at her before answering the Count.

"I find the red room cold, yes. It will be especially so by now."

Polly smirked as she leaned down to place the coffee before them. "You won't have no need of a fire, miss. Not with his lordship there."

Sylvia gasped in shock. The Count however merely threw his head back and laughed.

"That's enough now, Polly, you naughty girl!"

Polly glanced triumphantly at Sylvia and went out.

"I wish to retire," said Sylvia in a low voice. As she attempted to rise, the Count suddenly gripped her arm and drew her back down.

"Don't you think – you should be nice to me first?" he muttered.

"What do you mean?" asked Sylvia icily.

"I mean – this," said the Count.

In one swift move his lips were pressed heavily to hers.

Sylvia struggled but the Count pinned her arms to her side. She could smell the wax on his moustache and the wine on his breath.

"I will break you," he breathed. "I will make you mine tonight. You will never escape me then."

With almost superhuman force, Sylvia pushed the Count from her and leapt to her feet. Her eyes blazed so fiercely that for a moment the Count was distracted, gazing on her with fascination.

"You are a cad!" she cried. "I will have nothing more to do with you!"

"Oh, won't you?" sneered the Count. He made as if to rise but was so inebriated that he fell backwards at the first attempt.

Her breast heaving, keeping her gaze on him all the while, Sylvia edged towards the door. The Count's eyes were closing as they followed her.

"That's right – you go up – good girl – I'll come to you – soon."

His eyes closed and Sylvia almost cried out with relief as she realised he had fallen asleep.

She wrenched open the drawing room door and fled into the corridor and up the stairs. When she reached the red room, she turned the key hard in the lock behind her. Then she fell onto the bed and buried her head in the pillow.

She could not marry this man now that she had glimpsed his real character. He had lied to get her to Endecott. He had lied to get her into a vulnerable position. He was obviously unsure of her, afraid that she might change her mind despite the situation of her father. So he had hatched a plan to entrap her. Once he had ravished her, she would never be able to escape his clutches. She would be his wife then in all but name and the ceremony would be a mere formality.

What she could not understand was why he had gone to so much trouble. It could not be love that drove him, surely?

The wind howled at her through the door, through the cracks in the casement, down the chimney. She felt that it was laughing at her and it sounded like Polly. Ha ha ha. Ha ha ha.

Sylvia fell into an uneasy sleep.

*

"Sylvia! Open this door. Sylvia!"

Sylvia's eyes flew open at the sound of the Count's voice. He was rattling the doorknob violently.

"Let me in or you'll rue the day!"

Sylvia wondered wildly how much time had passed. The Count was no longer slurring his words and the wind seemed to have died down. The rain was lighter against the window.

"Let me in damn you or I'll take an axe to the door!"

Sylvia cowered on the bed, shivering violently. The doorknob twisted and turned a while longer and then she heard the thump of a fist on wood, before the Count raged off along the corridor.

Sylvia had no doubt but that he had gone for an axe. She knew that she could not hope for help from Polly. She was alone and in danger of losing her honour to a man she now utterly despised. She must gather her wits about her and find a way of escape.

She slipped from the bed and crossed to the window. Opening it she leaned out and immediately saw that a sturdy tree grew very close. One stout branch indeed almost grazed the glass.

There was no other way out for her.

Polly had taken her cape from her when she arrived so

there was nothing for it but to leave in what she was wearing.

She hesitated for a second and then tucked her skirts into her bloomers. Pushing the window wide she scrambled through onto the branch. It was wet and slippery but she held grimly on, edging her way towards the trunk. Here she was able to climb onto a lower branch and thus make her way slowly down the tree.

The lowest branch was still ten feet from the ground. Closing her eyes she let go and dropped.

Her foot twisted awkwardly under her as she landed, but the earth was soft from the hours of rain and she was not otherwise hurt. She lay for a moment winded.

Then from the red room above she heard the sound of an axe splitting wood. Terror spurred her on. She must find Columbine.

She limped to the back of the house, calling softly in the darkness. Soon she heard an answering whinny.

Columbine looked over a stable door as Sylvia approached. Sylvia opened the door and urged the horse out. There was no time to saddle her. She hauled herself onto the animal's back and thrust her hands deep into the mane.

"Go, Columbine, go," she whispered.

As if she had been longing all evening for this command, Columbine reared and set off at a gallop.

Horse and rider flew along the avenue of elms. The sky above was black and not a star was visible. The moon lay deep in cloud as if in mud. Mud flew from under the horse's hooves and splashed Sylvia's bloomers and skirt.

The rain, though it was lighter than before, still stung her face. She was soon frozen to the bone and her fingers were numb. Still she galloped on as if the very devil was after her.

She saw the gates of Endecott ahead. They were open. Beyond that the way ahead lay as dark as the way behind but she did not falter. She raced Columbine through the gates and onto the road.

Columbine's hooves struck sparks on the tarmacadum. The wind rose again, filling Sylvia's ears with its maddening shriek. She felt her grip on the mane weakening.

Her head bent low, she did not see the bend ahead. She did not see the lamp of a carriage as it hurtled towards her nor heard its wheels. Too late! Too late!

Columbine swerved at the last minute. Sylvia gave a cry as she was flung through the air. The world seemed to tumble over and over and then…she was aware of nothing more.

CHAPTER FIVE

Dappled shadows played on a yellow wall. Muslin curtains billowed at a long window, through which drifted the scent of rain-drenched lawns that were just beginning to dry. Doves cooed somewhere, and there was even the sudden high note of a peacock.

The room was peaceful. A vase of roses stood on a walnut table. Above the fireplace hung a scene from…from…

Sylvia could not remember. She closed her eyes again. She could not remember much at all, it seemed. She did not recognise this room. She did not know how she came to be here. All she could remember was being with her parents at Castle…Belham. Yes, she remembered that, and she remembered her name. *Sylvia.*

Suddenly she heard the sound of a door opening and closing gently, followed by the soft swish of silk. Someone had entered the room and was trying to move quietly about. Slowly Sylvia opened her eyes.

A tall, thin young lady with nut-brown hair was depositing a carafe of water and a glass on the walnut table. As she turned from her task, she caught Sylvia's puzzled gaze.

"Ah!" she said softly. "You are awake!"

This was all like some strange dream. "P..please

excuse me," whispered Sylvia, "but…I do not seem to know you or…this house."

"My name is Charity Farron," said the tall lady. "I am the sister of Lord Farron. You are at Farron Towers. You were brought here last night, unconscious."

"U..unconscious? W..why?"

"You do not remember?"

"N..no."

"You had an accident. You were riding along the road in pitch darkness and almost ran into our carriage. Your horse swerved violently at the last moment and you were thrown."

Sylvia gave a weak cry. "M..my horse. Columbine!"

"So that is her name?"

"Yes. Is she…?"

"She is fine," Charity reassured her. "She is out in the fields now enjoying the morning air. It is you we are concerned about. We do not know your name or where you are from."

"I am Sylvia, daughter of the Duke of Belham…"

"Ah! So you are resident at Castle Belham?"

"Y..yes."

"I will have a servant take a message to the castle. Your family must be concerned at your absence. You were heading towards Belham when you unhappily encountered us last night." Charity hesitated and then asked, in a careful tone. "May I ask – where you were coming from?"

Sylvia frowned. "I …don't seem able to remember."

"Try. It's important."

Sylvia's brow wrinkled with the effort. "I…remember that I sometimes ride out for the whole day. I often ride as far as the estuary."

Charity nodded. "You will not be surprised then to

learn that you can see the estuary from that window over there."

Sylvia looked towards the window. "So I was on my way home from this area…?"

Charity hesitated. "Yes, but I cannot believe you were simply returning from a day's ride. For one thing, it was very late, nearly midnight. For another your horse was not saddled and you were not wearing a cloak."

"No saddle? No cloak?" repeated Sylvia in wonder.

"No," affirmed Charity. "You seemed to be riding, as if pursued by somebody."

At this idea, Sylvia grew agitated. "But I…remember nothing of that," she said.

Charity looked at her with concern. "Well let us not worry about it at the moment. We have called for the local doctor to attend you. He should be here soon. Meanwhile perhaps you would care for some tea and toast?"

"Yes. Th..thank you," said Sylvia.

Charity smiled and made as if to move to the door.

"Charity?"

Charity turned. "Yes, Sylvia?"

"Who is 'we'? You keep saying 'we'."

Charity regarded Sylvia before answering. "I live here with my brother, Lord Farron. He and I were returning home together last night when our carriage almost ran into you. It was he who carried your unconscious body to the carriage and then rode your horse back to Farron Towers. We had to bring you here as we had no idea who you were. Now, let me get you some breakfast."

She had barely reached the door when Sylvia called out to her again.

"Charity…can you tell me…what is the subject of that painting? Over the fireplace?"

Charity looked up at the painting. "That? That is the Rape of Lucrece."

The Rape of Lucrece! Sylvia frowned as the door closed behind Charity. The Rape of Lucrece. She vaguely remembered the story and wondered why the title troubled her.

Her head fell back on the pillow. Trying to remember things made her tired. She should just relax her mind and see what happened.

She seemed to drift at first amidst pleasing images. Her room at Castle Belham. Papa riding beside her on Lancer. The wide, glittering estuary. Tompkins! Cook! Her step-mother looking delighted about something. Farther back in time she remembered…a London house with tartan wallpaper. A cat. Tilly! A garden at night…stars.

She frowned to herself. Her mind seemed to be full of unconnected memories. None of them helped explain why she had been out at night far from home, without a saddle and a cloak.

There was a knock at the door and a gentleman in black entered. He introduced himself as Doctor Glebe. Charity followed swiftly on his heels and with her a maid carrying a breakfast tray. The maid put the tray on the walnut table, her mouth open at the sight of the mystery girl, Sylvia.

"Leave the tray there, thank you, Hattie," said Charity.

Hattie backed out of the room, still agog.

Charity turned to Doctor Glebe. "You came sooner than expected, doctor."

"I happened to be in the vicinity on another call," explained the doctor. "I was on the road when your servant encountered me. Now tell me about our little friend here."

Charity went through the circumstances of the night before with the doctor. Sylvia listened dreamily.

"Well, she has a cut here under the hair-line," said the doctor, lifting loose curls from Sylvia's forehead. "She must have struck her head."

"We feared that," said Charity. "There is an upright stone at the side of the road where she fell, an ancient signpost."

The doctor nodded thoughtfully. "That accounts for the partial amnesia."

"Amnesia…" repeated Sylvia.

"That's right," said the doctor. He smiled down at her. "Before we talk about that, let me examine you to see if there are any broken bones."

Doctor Glebe's examination was thorough, and at the end of it he was able to reassure Sylvia that the only ill effect of her accident was the loss of memory.

"I have no doubt that it is not permanent," said the doctor. "Things will return to you slowly, piece by piece. In a few months you will have every detail of the jigsaw in place. Meanwhile you must rest for the next few days as the shock has no doubt weakened your constitution."

"Can I…go home?" asked Sylvia.

The doctor glanced at Charity. "It would be better not to move you immediately. If Lord Farron can extend his hospitality – "

"There is no question but that she must stay," cried Charity.

The doctor was reassured. He said that she should stay in bed for at least two days. He would check on her tomorrow. Charity thanked him and rang for Hattie to show him out.

"Now, Sylvia, shall I pour your tea?" she asked when Hattie and the doctor had gone. "You see we have an urn here so the pot is still warm."

Sylvia nodded. She felt thirsty and even a little hungry

suddenly. She drank two cups of tea and ate three slices of toast and marmalade. The food and drink revived her spirits. The doctor had said all she had to do was wait. Well, wait she would. She liked this pale yellow room with the muslin curtains and she liked Charity and her gentle manner. She could not help wondering about Lord Farron, though.

"When will I meet…your brother?" she asked.

Charity smiled. "He had to go to London this morning. He will return in a day or two. Then, if you are well enough to come down to supper, you will meet him. If it is not too clear a night, that is!"

Sylvia was puzzled. "Too clear a night?"

"Yes. Robert is something of an amateur astronomer. He has a telescope on the roof of the south tower. It is sometimes difficult to tear him away from the stars."

At the words 'astronomer' and 'stars' a wrinkle crossed Sylvia's brow. Some memory stirred, like a fish in the depths of a murky pool. Try as she might, however, she could not bring it to the surface. She gave up the attempt and lay back.

"Sleepy?" asked Charity.

"Y..yes. I suddenly…am."

Sylvia's eyes closed. She felt Charity draw the sheet up under her chin and then tiptoe softly from the room. After that, she was fast asleep.

*

The Duchess arrived in great consternation later that afternoon. She swept in her voluminous skirts up the stairs, Charity following, and into the yellow room where Sylvia lay. Her anxious, booming voice startled Sylvia awake.

"Sylvia! Darling gel!"

"Oh. Hello."

"*Hello*!" cried the Duchess. "Is that all you can say?

As if you'd just come in from a picnic! Where have you been, is what I want to know?"

"I'm afraid there is not much use asking her such questions," said Charity in a low voice. "Doctor Glebe said Sylvia is suffering from amnesia."

"Amnesia?" The Duchess looked startled. She moved in close to Sylvia and leaned over her. Her shiny face was only inches away from Sylvia.

"WHO AM I?" she boomed.

Sylvia shrank from her fierce gaze. "Why, you're…Mama."

"AND WHERE DO I BUY MY DUCK EGGS?"

Sylvia blinked. "F..Fortnum and Mason."

The Duchess, satisfied, drew herself up. "I don't call that amnesia!" she said to Charity.

Charity's lips twitched. "She remembers some things and not others," she said as simply as she could.

The Duchess frowned. "Well, does she remember that she has a sick father, who certainly shouldn't be worried in this way?"

"Father? Sick?" cried Sylvia, sitting up with a frantic air. "What is wrong with him?"

Charity shot a warning glance at the Duchess, who immediately understood that she was not to alarm the patient.

"Oh, it's really nothing to worry about," she said airily. "Just a bad chill. He'll feel so much better now he knows you are safe."

Sylvia lay back, reassured.

The Duchess drew Charity aside. "How very odd to remember about duck eggs – and not her father."

"The doctor said memories would come back to Sylvia in a fragmented way," whispered Charity. "At their own pace and in their own good time. Unless there was something she did not *wish* to remember. Something – traumatic."

"I'm sure I can't say what that could mean," said the Duchess haughtily. "We're a very normal and respectable family, you know. Nothing – *traumatic*, as you put it – ever happens to us. Unless you count the odd bill or two – and her father taking ill in the way he did."

Charity was silent for a moment. Instinctively she felt that she had to tread carefully with the Duchess, whose sense of propriety was obviously immense.

"Have you any idea at all – where Sylvia might have got to last night?" she asked at last, slowly and carefully.

"No idea at all!" said the Duchess.

She was being perfectly frank in her reply. No message had reached Castle Belham the night before to say that Sylvia was safe at Endecott, and this for one simple reason.

The stable boy entrusted with the message by Count von Brauer had never set out. Oh, he had meant to. He had gone to the stable, albeit reluctantly, and saddled his pony. He had taken his cap from its nail and his sou'wester from its hook. He had led the pony to the stable door and waited with her for a break in the thunder and lightning if not in the wind and rain, whistling a tune to cheer himself all the while. Oh, there was no doubt but that he intended to fulfil his commission. What he had not bargained for was the distraction of Polly.

Polly was a peach, she was. She had downy hair on her arms and a mole on her upper lip. She was plump as a partridge and oh, how her eyes could flash at a fellow when she wanted.

When Polly sidled into the stable with her hair all wet against her cheek, young Ben was astonished. He was even more astonished when she pressed her arms around him and asked if he would like to kiss her.

It was queer how time flew when a female set her cap at you!

By the time Ben had recovered his senses – and his cap, and his sou'wester – it was far too late to take a message to Castle Belham. Why, no-one at the castle would be up! He'd ride over straightaway at dawn and maybe then the Count would never know he hadn't executed his task at the correct time.

The Count did know, of course, because it was he who had sent Polly to detain young Ben. That way, the blame for the Duke of Belham not receiving a message to tell him where his daughter was that night would lie at the door of the stable boy and not that of the Count. The Count was anxious that a message not reach Belham *too soon*. Some intrepid servant might be asked to brave the storm and take a carriage to Endecott. After all, Sylvia was there without a chaperone!

So the Duchess was genuinely ignorant of Sylvia's whereabouts the night before. It never occurred to her that Sylvia might have visited Endecott unannounced precisely because she *was* without a chaperone. It was one thing for a young lady to roam the countryside on her own (though if truth were told the Duchess had never been reconciled to this habit of her step-daughter's) but quite another to spend the evening alone in her fiancé's house. Even if there *was* a storm! The Duchess of course could not guess at the manner in which the Count had tricked Sylvia into accompanying him to Endecott.

The Duchess had taken supper with her husband, in his rooms. She had sat with the Duke all evening. She usually went to say good-night to Sylvia on her way to her own room, but last night she had decided to remain with the Duke.

He had felt particularly frail all day and had not even

asked to see his daughter. The Duchess had asked Jeannie to make up a bed for her on the large sofa in the Duke's study. She asked Jeannie had Sylvia arrived home and Jeannie answered that she thought so but she hadn't taken supper.

Lady Sylvia often went straight to her own rooms when she came in and had a supper tray sent up. Before the Duchess could ask any more questions, the Duke had begun to groan in an alarming way. The Duchess hurried over to him to try to make him more comfortable. What with one thing and another she had forgotten all about Sylvia.

The note that had arrived from Endecott that morning had, therefore, come as a great shock. She felt horribly guilty not to have realised that her step-daughter had not made it home at all last night. As the Duke was sleeping deeply she sent for the carriage immediately and set off to fetch Sylvia. She did not wish to alert the Count until she had a better idea of what had might have befallen her step-daughter.

She was, however, thinking of the Count now as she looked on Sylvia. She was wondering whether or not to mention the Count to her step-daughter. Sylvia had not remembered that her father was ill. Perhaps she would also not remember that she was engaged to be married! Since she had never seemed easy about her impending marriage and had avoided meeting with the Count, it was more than likely that the subject was still rather tender with her. To introduce the subject might agitate her and impede her recovery.

The Duchess therefore decided she would say nothing for the moment, at least until she had spoken to the Count.

"Well, I'm sure we'll solve the mystery of where she was soon enough," sighed the Duchess.

Charity glanced at her quickly. "I do hope so because she was not in a happy state when we – encountered her," she ventured.

"No? Well, I'm sure the poor creature was soaked

through!" said the Duchess. "And terrified. It's no small matter to be out in a storm, you know."

"Oh, it was more than that," began Charity.

"But I'm sure it was nothing 'traumatic' as you suggest," said the Duchess, rising magisterially from the chaise. She had no wish to entertain thoughts of anything having happened – anything 'untoward' – that might throw the prospect of marriage to the Count into jeopardy. That would be too, too cruel. No, she was sure there was some innocent explanation for Sylvia's state the night before.

"Now," she continued. "I cannot allow myself to take up any more of your valuable time. If Sylvia can get dressed, I shall take the poor creature home at once in the carriage."

"I'm not sure that would be advisable," said Charity quickly. "Doctor Glebe suggested she should not be moved – at least for a while."

The Duchess put her hand to her breast. "But I couldn't possibly impose further upon your kindness – "

"I assure you, we are only too happy to look after her here. I shall make myself personally responsible for her well being."

The Duchess reflected. She had little aptitude for nursing and she knew it. It was quite enough, thank you, that she currently had to take care of the Duke. Charity Farron was a well bred young lady and Farron Towers the perfect place to recuperate. She, the Duchess, could organise the wedding much better without Sylvia's glum face around to discomfit her.

More importantly, it was perhaps better that Sylvia was not at Castle Belham for the Duke to ask her awkward questions, at least until the mystery of the previous evening was solved and, if necessary, dealt with.

"Well," she said briskly, "I shall gladly accept your offer. You will of course send for us when she is ready to return home? And you will not object if anyone should care to visit her here over the next few days?"

"Not at all," replied Charity.

The Duchess leaned forward and gave Sylvia a perfunctory kiss. Sylvia's eyes fluttered open.

"I am going, my dear," said the Duchess. "I believe I am leaving you in very capable hands!"

Sylvia smiled weakly. "You do indeed, Mama."

Charity accompanied the Duchess as far as the entrance hall, hoping to discover a little more about Sylvia. The Duchess, however, considering herself released from the constraints of duty, was now far too busy on her way out, noting the contents of Farron Towers to divulge anything of her step-daughter's life.

"Now *that* is a gem!" she cried, pausing before a porcelain shepherdess. "French, is it?" She turned the shepherdess upside down. "Oh, not French – "

She handed the statue to Charity to replace on the shelf from whence it had come and carried on. Further along the hallway her voice rose excitedly. "Oh, oh, oh! Forgive me, but that's a Reynolds isn't it? Splendid! We own one or two ourselves, though ours are in *gold* frames. They're up at our London house. Do *you* have a London address?"

"No. We stay with our god-mother, Lady Lambourne, when in town."

"*Lady Lambourne*! I know her. We have been to one or two of her balls. Oh my! That *must* be a portrait of an ancestor? I can see the likeness! She has the same eyes as you. And my goodness!" The Duchess stopped short just before the front door.

"We have the *exact same* Chippendale chair. Only we have a full set. Not just one. Ah, here is your maid with my coat. I am delighted that Sylvia finds herself in such *charming* quarters. Good-bye, good-bye! I shall see you again soon."

Charity was speechless as she gazed after the Duchess. "Well," she marvelled to herself. "I am absolutely none the wiser about your daughter now than I was before you arrived."

So little had been divulged that Charity was even unaware that the Duchess was not Sylvia's real mother!

*

Over the next two days Charity was as good as her word and took great care of Sylvia. She sat quietly at her bedside, busy with her embroidery but always alert to Sylvia's needs.

Tempting dishes were sent up to Sylvia from the kitchen. Strong broth, beef consommé, calves' foot jelly, platters of fruit, marzipan. Sylvia laughed and said she was being fattened up, like the children in Hansel and Gretel! Charity brought her interesting books from the library, books full of beautiful illustrations so that Sylvia's mental strength was not too taxed. If Sylvia felt very tired, Charity would read aloud to her.

Charity was delighted with Sylvia. She was deeply attached to her brother, but this was the first time she had enjoyed the constant companionship of someone her own age.

Soon the two young women felt as if they had known each other for years.

Memories returned slowly to Sylvia, seeming to flutter into her consciousness like butterflies. If she tried to seize them the minute they arrived, they vanished. If she waited, barely acknowledging them, they settled and she could examine them at her own leisure. Scene by scene her life returned to her.

There were some events, however, that still hovered beyond recall, though she was unaware of this. She did not remember the ball at Lady Lambourne's, nor the gentleman she had met in the garden. She did not remember the parlous state of her family's finances and she did not remember the night her father took ill. She remembered absolutely nothing at all about Count von Brauer.

It was as if he had ceased to exist. She remembered neither her first sight of him in the mist near the estuary, nor her subsequent introduction to him when he called at Castle Belham. She had no idea that she was engaged to be married to him and the terror of that night at Endecott was wiped as clean from her mind as chalk from a slate.

Sylvia recounted her returning memories to Charity, who was pleased to be able to put together a picture of her new friend's life. They discovered that they shared many interests in common. Charity, like Sylvia, was happier in the country than in the city. She had little interest in fashion or frivolous past-times. She loved nature and poetry and animals.

The first two nights Charity sat up with Sylvia, dozing in a large chair by her bed. On the third night however, Sylvia insisted that Charity go to her own room and get some proper rest. She felt so much stronger and calmer, she was sure she would be all right alone. Charity hesitated, but at last she admitted that she was very tired and would welcome a night in her own bed.

Left alone, Sylvia read for a while and then turned down the wick on the oil lamp. Bright moonlight flooded the room as she fell asleep.

The memory that would not come during her waking hours now seized its chance. Twisting into strange and unfathomable shape, it seeped insidiously into her sleeping mind.

She was running along a corridor. The walls were blood-red as were the floor and ceiling. She ran as if her life depended on it. Behind her was a shadowy pursuer, a man.

She could hear his panting breath, his wheedling tone. 'Stop, stop. There's a good girl! Stop!' She rounded a corner and her heart gave a lurch as she saw before her…a brick wall. She was trapped! Before she could turn she felt cold fingers around her neck and smelled, unaccountably, the odour of stale wine and hair wax…

Sylvia started up with a shriek. For a moment she could not remember where she was and this intensified her terror. She stared wildly round. There was a long window, a very pale light shining through a muslin curtain…shining around a dark, waiting figure.

With another scream Sylvia leapt from the bed. She raced to the door. Even as she glanced behind her she saw the curtain being drawn aside.

She was out in the corridor and running. Running as if to save her life. Her bare feet pattered on the deep carpet. Her night-dress fluttered about her. She had no idea where she was running to or from whom. Thus it was that, rushing around a corner, she found herself stumbling straight into the figure of a tall, astonished gentleman. Strong arms caught her as she fell with a sob.

"You are safe, madam. You are safe!"

Barely conscious as Sylvia was, the words reached her like balm. She felt herself lifted and carried back along the corridor. Pressing her face into this stranger's breast, she felt as if she could hear his heart beat.

Her rescuer kicked wide open the door to her room and carried her through.

She did not open her eyes until she was laid gently upon her bed. Then her eyelids fluttered as she looked up into a finely chiselled face, a lock of dark hair falling over a high, pale forehead, dark, passionate eyes gazing down upon her with a strange look of wonder.

For a second, his face was so close to hers their lips

might have met. Sylvia could feel his breath upon her cheek. Then, slowly, he straightened up from her. He struck a match and lit the wick of the bedside lamp.

"W..who are you?" murmured Sylvia.

He blew out the match before answering. "I am Lord Farron, madam. Brother of Charity."

Her senses no longer blunted by terror, hearing Lord Farron's voice clearly for the first time, Sylvia's heart gave a jolt. She was sure she had heard it somehow and somewhere before. But like so many other memories, the exact details eluded her.

For now, Lord Farron was part of the uncompleted jigsaw that seemed to be her past.

CHAPTER SIX

The crocuses were out and daffodils were bobbing merrily in the breeze. A bright April sun struck sparks off the estuary water.

Charity and Sylvia were strolling in the garden.

The air was crisp. Sylvia was glad that the Duchess had sent her over a cloak, as well as some dresses from Castle Belham.

Leaning on Charity's arm, Sylvia took a deep, happy breath. It was a beautiful day! The drama of the previous evening seemed to have taken place in another world entirely.

Lord Farron, once he had laid Sylvia on her bed, had rung for a maid. Poor Hattie, the only one to have heard the bell from her quarters behind the kitchen, arrived with her dress and apron thrown on in disarray and her night-cap still on her head. Lord Farron asked Hattie to summon his sister Charity.

Charity appeared minutes later in great concern. Lord Farron spoke to his sister quietly for a moment and then she hurried over to Sylvia's bedside. Sylvia stammered as she recounted her dream and her vision of a figure behind the curtain, which even now was billowing gently in the night breeze. Lord Farron went over to close the window. He assured both Charity and Sylvia that there was no sign of an intruder and Sylvia admitted that her imagination may well have run wild with fear.

Charity elected to remain with Sylvia. Lord Farron bowed and made his excuses. Sylvia's eyes followed him as he left the room.

Charity, tucking the sheets around Sylvia, explained that her brother had arrived home less than an hour ago. He had not wished to wake the household and had therefore stabled the horse that he had hired at the station himself and was on his way to his room when he encountered the distraught Sylvia.

Sylvia reddened. It did not escape her that on the two occasions she had met with Lord Farron, *she had ended up being carried in his arms*...

She was startled back to the present by Charity pointing out that they were now at the estuary's edge.

Wavelets, stirred up by the breeze, buffed at the earthen bank. A mother duck and her brood circled amid the reeds.

Sylvia, scanning the scene before her, remarked that there seemed to be no other house in the vicinity. Charity said that Farron Towers was indeed located in a lonely spot, although there was a manor called Endecott some five miles down the road.

"Oh," said Sylvia dreamily. "Who lives there?"

"The family that own it is abroad. At the moment it is being rented by a Count. He has been there some months."

Sylvia stooped to look at some bluebells. "Have you met him?" she asked.

Charity shook her head.

Sylvia straightened and stared across the estuary.

"That's where I used to ride a great deal," she suddenly pointed, "over there. I used to see your house and wonder who lived here. Were you brought up at Farron Towers? You and...your brother?"

"We have never lived anywhere else," smiled Charity. "It has been in my father's family for generations. It was left to my brother but he would not hear of me leaving. And to be sure, I have nowhere to go."

"What if…he marries?"

"I don't know," replied Charity. "But his god-mother says he is more interested in the motions of the stars than the ways of women!"

Laughing, the two young women made their way back to the house for breakfast.

Sylvia found herself disappointed that Lord Farron did not join them. She supposed he had travelled so far yesterday and arrived so late he wished to spend the morning in his rooms.

At midday a letter arrived from the Duchess. She wrote that all was well at the castle. She made no mention either of the Count or of the engagement.

Sylvia remained blissfully unaware of the fate that was still being arranged for her. At six o'clock Sylvia and Charity went to their separate rooms to dress for supper.

For the first time in her life, Sylvia found herself fretting about what to wear. If only the Duchess had sent a greater variety of her gowns from Castle Belham. There were only two here that she could possibly don – the midnight blue and the rose. She could not decide which suited her best. In the end she decided on the midnight blue – it seemed more sophisticated.

She sat at the mirror arranging her hair this way and that, feeling at a great disadvantage. She had none of her combs here! None of her jewellery! Not even the tiniest bottle of perfume!

She leaned closer to the glass. Her eyes shone back at her like moonstones. She pinched her cheeks – just as the Duchess used to pinch them – and moistened her lips. Yes, she decided, she would pass. She *was* pretty. Look at how her hair gleamed in the lamp-light like a cornfield in the sun.

Suddenly she blushed and lowered her eyes from her own image.

Why was she taking such unaccustomed care with her appearance?

As she descended the stairs later her heart began to beat so loudly, she was sure the sound must resound through the house like...why, like the boom of the supper gong that was even now being struck!

"Why, Sylvia, how lovely you look!" exclaimed Charity as Sylvia entered the dining room. "Doesn't she, Robert?"

"Indeed she does," responded Lord Farron. Sylvia was startled by his searching gaze. It was as if he was hoping for something from her...some word, some look...that she could not give. He came forward to lead her to her seat. Her small, white hand rested on his arm like a little bird.

She found it difficult to concentrate on her food. There was turtle soup and artichoke and trout and crushed fruit with meringue, but she could hardly tell one dish from the other. Her eyes kept straying to the figure of Lord Farron.

His had such a strong, intelligent face. There was a great deal of reserve in his manner, but also a latent power that thrilled Sylvia to the bone.

She felt he was like no other man she had ever met.

Lord Farron was talking about his recent visit to London on business.

"On my way back to King's Cross station, I dropped in at Culworth's Antiquarian bookshop," he said casually.

"It would have been more unusual if you had *not* dropped in at Culworth's," teased Charity. She turned to Sylvia. "I'm beginning to think there must be a Miss

Culworth behind the dusty counter somewhere."

Sylvia gave a quick, unhappy smile.

"But there is!" said Lord Farron soberly. "She is the shape of a beehive and has whiskers on her chin. Alas, I can't get near her for admirers!"

Charity gave a merry laugh.

"Lord Farron," said Sylvia in a low voice, "you are…very interested in..the stars, I think?"

Lord Farron regarded her sharply. "I could imagine – no greater passion – until recently," he said, and looked away.

Charity looked startled. She gazed at her brother thoughtfully for a moment and then turned to Sylvia.

"You know that Lord Farron has a telescope on one of the tower roofs?" she reminded Sylvia.

"Yes. I remember you telling me," replied Sylvia. "It must be…wonderful…to see the stars in the sky at closer quarters."

"Indeed it is!" declared Charity. "And I'm sure Robert would be only too delighted to let you use his telescope."

Lord Farron inclined his head. "As soon as we have a cloudless night," he promised.

Sylvia found herself wishing vehemently that such a night would arrive soon.

The following morning she watched from her window as Lord Farron went for a ride. He looked very confident on his black stallion. He returned just before eleven. She heard him call to the stable boy to take his horse and felt herself blush at the sound of his voice.

A little while later Hattie knocked on the door and handed her a vase full of pink, dew-drenched roses. Sylvia gasped in delight.

"Who sent these?" she asked.

Hattie rocked from side and side, grinning. "They'se from the Master, miss."

"Lord...Farron?"

Hattie nodded and bobbed and went away with the grin still on her face.

Sylvia took the vase over to the fireplace and placed it on the mantelpiece. Glancing up as she arranged the roses to her liking, her eyes alighted on 'The Rape of Lucrece,' and she gave an involuntary shudder.

Why did that painting so disturb her, even when she was in such a contented mood as now?

She thanked Lord Farron profusely when she saw him at lunch. He bowed and said the flowers had come from the Farron rose garden, which was famous in the district. Their delicate colour, he added, had reminded him of her.

Sylvia's breath seemed to catch in her throat.

That afternoon Lord Farron drove Charity to town to procure provisions. Sylvia was supposed to rest but she found her mind swooping and soaring like a skylark. As soon as she heard the sound of the carriage wheels returning from the station, she leapt to her feet and ran downstairs.

Lord Farron turned to watch her as she descended the stairs. She did not know it, but her eyes were bright as stars and a delicate flush rose in her cheeks as her eyes met his.

Charity, who was removing her travelling coat, noticed the direction of her brother's gaze and gave a little half-smile to herself.

At supper Lord Farron informed the two young women that as the sky was very clear that night, he would like to invite them to view the stars.

The stairs to the tower were steep and slippery. It was a long and arduous climb. The last step before the summit was particularly deep and Lord Farron turned to help Sylvia.

She felt dizzy at the touch of his hand.

From the tower roof one could see a faint gleam on the estuary water, but all else was in darkness.

Sylvia gasped when she looked through the telescope. She had never seen the stars so clearly. Lord Farron stood at her elbow, leaning down to her as he explained the night sky.

"There, to the north west, is Castor and Pollux, the twins of Gemini. Over there is the Plough. And you see that swathe of stars? That is the Milky Way."

"It is all so beautiful," breathed Sylvia.

Lord Farron watched her keenly. The name of another star was on his tongue – he seemed to hesitate a moment – and then he plunged on.

"That star there, to the east, you may be acquainted with already. It is called Arcturus – the Pathfinder."

Sylvia's head jerked up.

"*Arcturus the Pathfinder…*" she repeated. She looked from Lord Farron to the star and back to Lord Farron, all the while a puzzled little frown on her brow. Suddenly her eyes widened and her hands flew to her cheeks.

"It is you!" she breathed.

Lord Farron gave a deep bow, his eyes never leaving her face. "Yes. It is I!"

Bewildered, Sylvia looked from brother to sister.

"Have you known…all along?"

Lord Farron's voice was full of deep emotion as he spoke. "The night of the accident – it was very dark. You were in such a dishevelled state when I found you, all covered in mud, your hair loose around your face – that I simply did not recognise you. I carried you in great haste to the carriage and in great haste from the carriage to the house – but once you were ensconced in the room you now inhabit, I naturally left you to the ministrations of my sister. The next morning I was obliged to go to London. It was only when I encountered you two nights later – wandering in the corridor, that I recognised you. My sister had of course learned who you were by then. We decided not to tell you, but to see if the memory returned naturally."

Here Lord Farron hesitated, scanning Sylvia's face with great feeling. "I am most happy, madam," he added in a lower tone, "to discover that you had not forgotten me. For believe me, I had never forgotten you."

Sylvia felt faint. Every detail of that evening at Lady Lambourne's seemed now to rush in upon her. The ball…the garden…the gentleman in the mask kneeling to put on her satin shoe. Even more, she remembered how she had wished to see him again.

How little could she have imagined that her wish would come so spectacularly true!

*

Over the next few days Lord Farron spent every spare moment of his time with Sylvia. He and she read together, strolled in the garden together, played cards together. Charity, who was of course always with them, teased that she was cast aside for her brother and had merely the occupation of chaperone.

Doctor Glebe came every day to check on his patient. Lord Farron questioned him anxiously after each visit and was relieved to be told that the doctor was pleased with Sylvia's progress, although concerned that there were still such gaps in her memory about her accident.

Sylvia might have reflected more on that odd evening from the past, had she not been so happy in the present. If anyone – Lord Farron, Charity, the doctor – even gently encouraged her to try and remember, a strange, dark lassitude came over her. During such times she began to tell herself a story that fitted the events of that night.

She had stayed out too late – she had been caught out

in the storm – she had sheltered somewhere – she had then made a mad dash for home, which resulted in being thrown from her horse.

Gradually this passed in her mind for the truth.

Eventually Doctor Glebe concluded that so many days had elapsed since the accident, it was now possible that Sylvia would never remember the details of that night.

The memory had sunk beyond retrieval.

This prognosis was relayed to the Duchess of Belham.

The Duchess, busy with preparations for the wedding, had not visited Farron Towers again although she had kept in contact by letter.

She had no idea of the burgeoning relations between her step-daughter and Lord Farron.

One morning Lord Farron had to go to the local town on business. Charity accompanied him. Sylvia said that she could perfectly well occupy herself alone until noon.

It was a warm and pleasant afternoon, so she took a book and went to seat herself in the orchard.

She was reading quietly in the sun when a figure appeared amidst the trees.

It was Count von Brauer.

He stood for a moment watching Sylvia, twirling the end of his moustache between thumb and forefinger.

Count von Brauer had been consumed with rage after the flight of Sylvia. If only he had succeeded in forcing himself upon her! Run as she might after that, she would have been his! She would have held her tongue out of shame and she would have married him as planned, because he would have rendered her unfit to marry anyone else!

He had realised from the first that he repulsed Sylvia. This troubled him not a jot. Such was his nature that he even derived pleasure from seeing her flinch with distaste before him. It had begun to dawn on him, however, that should her revulsion overcome her sense of duty, Sylvia might withdraw from the engagement. For reasons that he divulged to no-one, this would never do! There was too much at stake and he could not hurry the marriage without arousing suspicion. He had resolved therefore to entice Sylvia to Endecott and secure her to him by nefarious means.

Not for the first time, the fruit of the vine had ruined his plans. He had drunk too much and lost his advantage.

Certain that he would be summoned to Castle Belham to account for his behaviour, he had paced the corridors of Endecott endlessly. He was not sure of what to do. Should he pack his bags and leave? Or stay and brazen it out? Would there be any point to brazening it out? Surely, however he defended himself, there would be no question of a marriage now?

He was gulping down a glass of whiskey when he saw, through the window, the Belham coach roll up to Endecott.

He stiffened when the Duchess entered the drawing room but was then astonished when she offered him her hand to kiss. He listened in disbelief as, hardly stopping to draw breath, she recounted the details of her hurried visit that afternoon to Farron Towers.

At the end he fell back in his chair and stared at the Duchess.

"Amnesia?" he repeated in wonder.

"That's right," said the Duchess. "And very selective it is too."

She hesitated. The Count must eventually hear the details of that night and she wanted to plant an acceptable scenario into his head.

"The prevailing opinion is," she went on, "she got lost in the storm. She probably tried to shelter somewhere, in a barn or abandoned stable. She took the saddle off to rest her horse and removed her own cloak to dry it. Then something frightened her – an animal, most likely – and she took off again with disastrous results."

The Count's moustache twitched with amusement as he grasped what the Duchess was up to.

"That is surely the explanation," he nodded gravely. He sighed. "If only she had thought of coming to me. I am not so far from the road where the accident occurred."

"Oh, if only she had," agreed the Duchess.

She did not remain long at Endecott. She wanted to return to Castle Belham before the Duke became too agitated. The Count walked her to her carriage and kissed her hand before she mounted.

"It is probably advisable for the moment," said the Duchess, "that you do not visit Sylvia. Better to let her regain her strength."

The Count watched her carriage leave and then walked back to the house in a daze. What unbelievable luck! Amnesia!

He was still in with a chance. Until, that is, Sylvia's memory of that night returned.

If it returned!

The Duchess's prescription that he not visit Sylvia until she regained her strength had at first suited him. Why appear and possibly jolt her memory? Better to wait and see.

Then, this very morning, he received the message from the Duchess informing him that Doctor Glebe believed Sylvia was now unlikely to remember more than she already had.

It was time to reclaim his fiancée!

He had saddled his horse and ridden over to Farron Towers. Hoping on such a fine day to find Sylvia somewhere outside – and on her own – he had tethered his horse beyond the gates and walked into the estate, keeping to the shade of the trees. Circling the house carefully, he had glimpsed her sitting in the orchard. Alone! Luck was with him all right!

It was at this point that Sylvia looked up from her book and espied him there. She shaded her eyes with her free hand, trying to discern who this unfamiliar figure might be.

Count von Brauer came jauntily down the path and bowed.

"Good-morning, madam," he said.

"G..good morning," replied Sylvia.

The Count whistled a little as he regarded her. Sylvia glanced quickly around, suddenly uneasy.

"You don't know me then?" asked the Count.

"N..no, sir. I don't."

"Or rather, let's say, you don't *recognise* me?"

Sylvia paled. "Do you mean…I *should* know you?"

"Oh, you should. Indeed you should." The Count began to whistle again. He was rather enjoying the situation.

Sylvia looked up at him, perplexed.

"Were we…well acquainted?" she asked falteringly.

The Count stopped whistling. He regarded her thoughtfully. Better be careful here. Play his cards right. Mustn't alienate her. What he needed to do was get her on his side and then hurry this wedding along.

"My dear Lady," he said in as soft a tone as he could muster, "we were most intimately and legitimately acquainted. Your step-mother herself will enlighten you."

"My step-mother? She has said nothing that indicated such a friendship existed between myself and…any other."

The Count adopted an expression of deep concern. "Ah! My dear Sylvia! We wished to let you gently recover your memories. But alas! I see that you have forgotten your devoted friend."

Here he trailed off, shaking his head mournfully.

Sylvia felt helpless. "And what is…my devoted friend's name?"

The Count hesitated. Here was the crucial moment. Would the sound of his name quicken memories that he would prefer to lie buried forever?

"I am – Count von Brauer," he said slowly.

Even as he spoke Sylvia turned her head sharply. Was that the sound of coach wheels? She thought so, she *hoped* so!

"Madam?" the Count prompted her with a frown.

She turned back to him. "I'm sorry, I…"

"*Count von Brauer,*" repeated the Count, endeavouring to hide his annoyance.

Sylvia shook her head, near to tears. Why could she not remember this man?

"Sir, tell me please, for the love of God…what were you to me, or I to you?"

The Count drew in his breath. She did not remember. He was, for the moment, quite safe. If he could marry her within the fortnight, he was surely home and dry.

He leaned down and took up her hand from where it lay in her lap. She shrank away as he raised it to his lips.

"I was your future and you were mine," he replied.

Sylvia stared at him, aghast. Could he mean what she thought? Heavens, let it not be so.

As if to compound her misery and confusion, she heard at that moment the voice of Lord Farron as he approached the orchard.

"Sylvia! We are returned."

He stopped short as he saw that she was not alone. Then he came more slowly towards her. He bowed civilly to the Count, but as he straightened and looked more fully upon him, his brow suddenly furrowed.

Sylvia felt it incumbent upon her to make an introduction.

"This is…Count von Brauer," she said unhappily.

"Your servant," said Lord Farron stiffly to the Count.

He turned to Sylvia. "My humble apologies, madam. Had I known you were not alone, I should not have intruded upon yourself and your friend."

"Oh, ha!" exclaimed the Count. "You are mistaken, sir, if you think me a friend of this young lady."

Sylvia was shocked. Lord Farron regarded the Count in amazement.

"What the deuce do you mean, sir?"

"Oh," shrugged the Count coolly, "what I mean is that I am no *mere* friend of this pretty lady. I am rather the man privileged to be her future husband."

Lord Farron seemed to reel back as if struck. He was utterly speechless.

Sylvia, stunned, stared at the ground.

The Count took hold of the end of his moustache and rolled it between his fingers, his eyes narrowed. He had seen Lord Farron's reaction and recognised it immediately for what it was. The reaction of a man who suddenly discovers he has a rival.

Sylvia lifted her head at the soft cooing of a wood pigeon. Everything – the orchard, the house, the estuary, looked as it had five minutes ago, but *her* world had changed irrevocably.

The Count felt he had ventured enough for now. He took hold of Sylvia's hand again. Lord Farron flinched and turned away. The Count expressed his desire to visit Sylvia tomorrow. She looked up at him and nodded miserably. She did not know how she could refuse. The Count then bowed to Lord Farron and set off along the path.

It was Lord Farron who spoke first. "What do you

know of – your fiancé?"

She looked up, startled. Was Lord Farron under the impression that she had remembered from the first that she was engaged, but had said nothing to either him or Charity?

"N..nothing. How could I…?"

Lord Farron snapped a twig from a nearby bough in two.

"Are you in love with him?" he asked abruptly.

Sylvia's head swam. How could she know if she were in love with a man she did not remember? At the same time, she felt her fate was sealed. She had just learned that she had a fiancé. It was news that rendered her desolate, but she had no doubt of where her duties now lay. It was not for her to reveal her unhappiness at the situation.

"I c..cannot remember," she stammered, "but anyway I am told…that love grows once you are…wed."

Lord Farron wheeled on her with a face full of bitterness. "That, madam, depends on who you marry!" he growled. Without another word he gave a curt bow and walked away.

Sylvia stared after his retreating figure, feeling as if all the hope, all the light of her life, went with him.

CHAPTER SEVEN

Count von Brauer lost no time in informing the Duchess of his impromptu visit to Farron Towers. He was anxious to impress upon her the desirability of removing her step-daughter from the company of the dashing Lord Farron.

"After all," he shrugged, watching the Duchess closely, "Sylvia does not remember me and – she is in a highly susceptible state at the moment."

The Duchess was so distracted by this intimation of an unwelcome friendship between Sylvia and Lord Farron, that she quite forgot to rebuke the Count for visiting Sylvia without her express command. The Duchess was sure that Lord Farron, though of an old and distinguished family, was by no means as wealthy as the Count. The Count, after all, owned vast estates in Bavaria!

She must act quickly or all would be lost!

She sent a message to Sylvia announcing that she would be coming to fetch her home later that day.

At Farron Towers, meanwhile, Charity and Sylvia sat down to lunch without Lord Farron. Hattie said he had gone out on his horse and would not return till late. Sylvia, head low, sat toying with her food. Charity glanced at her now and then from under her brows.

Charity was aware that something had occurred between her brother and Sylvia, something that had rendered them both equally miserable. For the moment neither of them wished to enlighten her on the subject and she respected their silence even as it troubled her.

A hundred times, Sylvia was on the point of telling her friend what had happened and a hundred times she held her tongue. She could not bear it if the same bitter look crossed Charity's face at the news as had crossed Lord Farron's.

It was during dessert that a message for Sylvia was brought in on a tray.

Sylvia went pale as she read the message. Then she burst into tears and rushed from the table.

Charity went after her in alarm. When she tapped on Sylvia's door, however, Sylvia simply called out in a choked voice that she was obliged to prepare to return home. She offered no further explanation for her tears and Charity retired, hurt and puzzled.

An hour later, her cheeks still damp, Sylvia sat disconsolately at her window. She stared out at the green sward of lawn that ran down to the estuary. Her heart was so heavy she could imagine it sinking like a stone into those grey-green waters.

She had been so happy here at Farron Towers, so happy in the company of Lord Farron and his sister. It was in all innocence that she had allowed herself to feel more for Lord Farron than was, as it turned out, appropriate. Yet still she berated herself.

How could the fact that she was engaged to be married have been so completely wiped from her mind?

When she thought of the Count her heart gave a wild, unhappy lurch. In what circumstances had she accepted his proposal of marriage? Could she ever have been in love with him and if so, would that love return with her memory of him?

She assumed the Count had informed the Duchess of

his visit that morning and that was why her stepmother was coming to fetch her home.

It was time for her to resume those duties that fell upon an engaged young lady!

Feeling a sob rise in her throat she pressed her handkerchief to her lips. It would not do to let Lisbeth hear her cry.

Lisbeth, Charity's lady's maid, was in the room packing Sylvia's trunk.

"Shall I put this shawl in or will you wear it on your journey?" asked Lisbeth.

Sylvia looked at the white shawl dully. "Oh – put it in the trunk. I'll wear my cloak home."

At that moment she heard the sound of carriage wheels on the cobbles below. She quickly dried her eyes and rose from the window.

"It's all packed now, my lady," said Lisbeth. "I'll have it carried down to the hall right away."

"Thank you," said Sylvia. She moved to the door just as a soft knock sounded on the other side.

It was Charity.

Charity regarded her friend anxiously. "Your stepmother has arrived," she said.

Sylvia had long since enlightened Charity as to her true relationship with the Duchess.

Sylvia nodded and looked away. "I know. I am going down now. Has...Lord Farron...returned from his ride?"

Charity shook her head.

Sylvia's sense of desolation was immense.

She had longed to see his face just one more time before she left.

The two young women descended the stairs together in silence.

Sylvia still could not bring herself to tell Charity about her sudden discovery that she had a fiancé.

Lord Farron would tell his sister soon enough.

The Duchess greeted Sylvia and Charity coolly in the hallway below. She made it clear she had no desire to loiter at Farron Towers and ordered Sylvia's trunk to be immediately loaded on to the carriage.

She was secretly shocked at Sylvia's stricken expression and surmised she was whisking her step-daughter away not a moment too soon.

Charity and Hattie went out onto the steps to bid them farewell.

The coach driver handed the Duchess in. Sylvia turned and clung for a moment to Charity.

"S..say good-bye to…your brother for me," she whispered.

At that moment there came the sound of hooves on the road to the house.

Sylvia swung round to see Lord Farron galloping almost recklessly into view.

Rather than take the curve east of the drive he urged his horse over the orchard gate and on through the trees. Sylvia's hand flew to her throat. The Duchess, leaning from the coach to see what was going on, gave a frown.

Lord Farron pulled up with a loud 'whoa' and leapt from his horse. His face was pale, despite his ride, as his eyes took the scene in at a glance.

"You – are leaving?" he asked breathlessly.

"Yes," murmured Sylvia.

"Come along," the Duchess scolded Sylvia, "I must get back to your father."

Lord Farron turned and quickly bowed to the Duchess. "I trust – the Duke of Belham's health is improved?" he enquired politely.

"Vastly," replied the Duchess coldly," especially since he knows his daughter will be secure under his roof tonight."

Charity started in astonishment. "She has been secure enough under our roof, I would hope!' she said with some heat.

"Oh, indeed, I am all thanks," replied the Duchess. "But such a young gel is better off under her parents' eye, you know."

Charity said nothing more. Lord Farron held out his hand to help Sylvia into the coach. She trembled at his touch. The Duchess watched all the while with pursed lips.

Sylvia leaned forward in her seat to speak to Lord Farron at the still open door.

"You will…bring Charity to visit me…at Belham?"

Before Lord Farron could reply the Duchess spoke out. "Oh, but you won't be at Belham, my dear. Not for a while. Tomorrow we go up to London to put together your trousseau. Your brothers-in-law have most generously offered to pay."

With that, the Duchess signalled to the waiting coach driver to slam the door. Sylvia caught one last glimpse of Lord Farron's anguished gaze before the driver's whip cracked through the air and the coach jolted into motion.

*

It was very warm for a day in early May. All the windows in the Belham's Mayfair house were flung wide open.

Sylvia sat on her bed in her petticoat, her arms locked around her drawn-up knees. Edith and Charlotte were busy opening all the packages that had been carried up from the coach a few minutes before.

For seven frantic days, Sylvia had been dragged from

one fashionable boutique to another. She had been dressed and undressed in every fitting room in London. Edith and Charlotte had held up exquisite garment after exquisite garment – satin corsets, silk lingerie, velvet stockings, embroidered hats. They were bitterly disappointed that Sylvia showed so little appetite for this most delectable of pursuits – shopping! Such was her disinterest that it was they who ended up choosing her wardrobe each day.

"Just look at these shoes!" cried Edith. "Look at those tiny rosebuds stitched on the strap. Delectable!"

Charlotte took a huge straw hat out of a cocoon of tissue. "Oh, my – imagine this at afternoon tea at Kumpfners."

Sylvia dropped her chin onto her knees and stared at the counterpane. Kumpfners was the hotel on the Rhine at which the Count had suggested they spend a delayed honeymoon in September, on their way to his Bavarian estates.

The whole idea of the wedding and the life that would come after, filled Sylvia with horror but she had been made well aware of where her duty lay. It had not taken the Duchess long to re-acquaint Sylvia with the imperatives of this marriage. Edith and Charlotte never wasted a moment in reminding her that it was probably saving her father's life.

One or two hazy memories of the Count had returned to Sylvia, such as his first visit to Castle Belham, and the day she encountered him in the mist near the estuary. She still had no memory whatsoever of the night she had fled from Endecott. Nevertheless, she harboured an instinctive dislike of the Count and barely permitted him to touch her.

He, worried that at any moment she might remember his attempt to ravish her, pressed now for a hastier marriage than planned. He cited Sylvia's obvious attraction to Lord Farron as the reason. Better to let him, the Count, marry Sylvia and take her away from England for a month or two.

A new husband could soon banish all thoughts of another man.

The Duchess, though regretting her plans for a huge county wedding, felt obliged to agree.

The wedding was now set for three weeks hence, during the first week of June.

Sylvia felt helpless, impelled towards the altar on a tide of dresses, shoes, hats, bloomers – impelled on a tide of money, money that would no doubt buoy up the Belham fortunes for generations to come.

She had received various letters of congratulations but nothing from Lord Farron. Charity had sent a short, polite note. Otherwise an unnatural silence prevailed between the two erstwhile friends.

Sylvia lifted her eyes at an exclamation from Edith. Her sister was in the process of drawing a white fur coat from its box.

"Oh," breathed Charlotte. "This is divine. Imagine wearing it on a sleigh, driving round your Bavarian estates."

The two sisters, eyes moist with romantic longings, rushed over and draped the fur around Sylvia's shoulders. They clapped their hands as they gazed on her.

"The little Princess!" sighed Edith.

"Countess!" Charlotte corrected her.

Sylvia shrugged off the coat.

"Oh, can't you be even a *little* bit enthusiastic!" complained Charlotte.

"You're like a – a wet fish!" joined in Edith. "Won't you *enjoy* having all these lovely things?"

"Not if the price is marrying Count von Brauer," riposted Sylvia bitterly.

The sisters raised their eyes to the ceiling.

"Such ingratitude!"

"You're just being stubborn."

"You're going to be very happy with him!"

"Just wait and see."

Sylvia said nothing. Her sisters, having unpacked everything from their boxes, rushed off to refresh themselves before tea. They would send a maid to put everything away for Sylvia.

Sylvia's eyes slowly took in the room, the discarded items, the mounds of lingerie, the dresses flung over the chaise. She sighed and put her hand over her face.

If only all this had been for a marriage to *someone else!*

She was disturbed from her reveries by the sound of a carriage drawing up outside the house. She wondered who it might be at this hour of the afternoon. Not the coach to take her sisters home. They were staying to supper and then accompanying the Duchess with Sylvia and the Count to Lady Lambourne's birthday party. Not so her brothers-in-law, who were both away attending to matters at their country estates.

She leaped up when she recognised the voice that was ordering the coach driver to wait.

It was the voice of Lord Farron!

Sylvia had learned that both Charity and her brother were the god-children of Lady Lambourne. She had simply not allowed herself to hope that Lord Farron would come to London for his god-mother's birthday party.

Yet here he was, not just in London, but at Sylvia's own door!

She rushed around the room as the heavy door bell rang. Where was her dressing-gown...her dress...anything more seemly than her bodice and petticoat? She couldn't appear at the window in those!

Hearing the front door open she ran to the bed and

caught up the white fur. Drawing it around her she hurried to the window and pulled back the curtain.

There were voices below but she could not make out what was being said. She leaned further out.

She could see Lord Farron below. Her heart caught in her throat. Then she heard him being asked to wait. *Asked to wait*! Without inviting him in?

Lord Farron bowed. He turned and stood at the top of the steps, looking down the street.

Dare she call down to him? No, no, that was simply not appropriate behaviour.

Yet how she longed for him to see her and address her.

He turned. Someone had come back to the front door. There were low words. Lord Farron seemed to stiffen. He gave a curt bow and stepped away, crumpling something in his hand. For an instant he glanced up and his eyes alighted on Sylvia's fur-swathed figure at the window. He gave no sign of greeting to her, but turned on his heels and went swiftly down the steps.

Without another backward glance he got into the coach and drove off.

The clip clop of his horses' hooves seemed to ring in Sylvia's ears long after his coach had turned the corner and disappeared…

*

"Oh, being engaged must suit you, my dear! You look perfectly splendid."

Sylvia, in a shimmering pink voile dress, bobbed a curtsey to Lady Lambourne.

"You made quite an impression on my god-daughter, Charity," continued Lady Lambourne with a twinkle. "You were almost the sole topic of her letters for a while."

Sylvia flushed. "Is…is Charity here?"

"Goodness me, no. You can never prise Charity away from the countryside. She's quite the little hermit, you know."

Sylvia would have liked to ask about Lord Farron but the Count was at her side.

Neither the Duchess nor Sylvia's step-sisters had cared to discuss Lord Farron's visit to the Belham house that afternoon. The Duchess had brushed the topic aside when Sylvia mentioned it. *It had been an inopportune visit and she had had to let him know so.* Now, would Sylvia please concentrate on choosing a colour for her sisters' dresses, or had she quite forgotten they were to be her matrons of honour?

Sylvia did not venture to bring the subject up again.

All that mattered was that Lord Farron was in London.

Surely she would see him that evening at his god-mother's party?

The Duchess, Edith and Charlotte all exclaimed at the sound of music striking up in the ballroom. Though there were fewer guests here tonight than there had been at the annual ball, Lady Lambourne had still provided a full orchestra.

"One does not reach such a venerable age every day," she exclaimed.

"And may I ask exactly *how* venerable that might be?" smiled the Count.

"Certainly not, you wicked, wicked man!" cried Lady Lambourne, smacking his arm with her fan. "But if you are not averse to leading such a grandmama onto the floor, do offer me a dance during the evening. I want to find out all about you, since you are snaffling up one of the prettiest girls of the season."

The Count bowed. "With great pleasure, ma'am."

Lady Lambourne moved on to other guests. The

Count led the Belham women into the ballroom.

Sylvia's eyes flickered quickly over the dancing couples. He was not one of them! She was almost glad. If he had been one of them, it could only have been because he was dancing with some other young lady!

She agreed to a waltz with the Count. His fingers pressed hard into her back until she almost winced. She would not meet his eye. She was relieved that he had promised the second dance to Edith.

The Duchess and Charlotte had partners. Before Sylvia should find herself asked to dance by anyone else, she slipped out of the ballroom.

She wandered through the house, ostensibly without purpose, yet always alert for a sight of Lord Farron.

He was not in the drawing room with the ladies nor in the library with the gentlemen. He was in none of the corridors. At last, heart beating expectantly, she walked out into the garden. Perhaps he was actually waiting for her here!

But the garden lay silent and empty under the cloudy night sky.

Disappointed, Sylvia strolled along the terrace and re-entered the house through a different French window.

This was the room where the drinks were being served. A large, silver bowl of punch sat on a table.

Lord Farron was coming away from the table with a glass of punch in his hand.

Happily, Sylvia moved towards him. She had almost reached his side when he glanced her way. Recognition flared in his eyes, but before she could even so much as raise her hand in greeting, an expression of such utter coldness, such icy indifference, fell on his face that she was stalled in her tracks.

"L..Lord Farron," she murmured.

He bowed – muttered, "Lady Sylvia" coldly – and moved on.

Sylvia stood, stunned. Her eyes followed Lord Farron as he joined the company of a trim, elegant woman with coils of jet black hair. He handed this woman the glass of punch that he had procured and her eyes flashed as she thanked him. Sylvia stepped back in dismay as she saw the woman put a hand on Lord Farron's arm.

She turned and stumbled back out onto the terrace and down the steps to the garden. She ran all the way down to the fountain and stood there panting, staring into the dark water.

What had she done to make him greet her so coldly, so cruelly? She had so hoped they might continue to be friends, even after her marriage. She had never, she was sure, betrayed that she felt anything *other* than friendship for him. So why should he now so spurn her?

Miserable and bewildered, she hardly registered that the weather had changed and the air was now growing chill. It was only when she found herself shivering violently that she reluctantly returned to the house.

She almost crept through the rooms, convinced that everyone had noticed Lord Farron's cold rejection of her. She wished she could disappear into some mouse-hole or coal scuttle!

"Sylvia!"

It was Edith.

"Sylvia, I'm leaving. I've ordered a separate carriage. If you wish to come with me and stay at my house tonight meet me in a few minutes at the front door."

Edith sailed off without another word.

Sylvia hurried to the ballroom. She must tell Mama and Charlotte and the Count that she was leaving with Edith.

But the Duchess and Charlotte were spinning merrily

around on the floor with their respective partners. The Count was nowhere to be seen.

Sylvia tried desperately to catch the eye of either the Duchess or Charlotte but they whirled on obliviously.

Sylvia waited for a few seconds hoping the music would end, but it seemed to go on and on.

At this rate Edith would leave without her.

She decided to look for the Count. She suspected that he might be in the library, smoking. He was indeed there, playing cards. She hesitated, unwilling to approach. Suddenly she heard the music in the ballroom end. There came the sound of scattered applause. Now was her chance. Turning on her heels she ran all the way back and reached the Duchess and Charlotte as they were leaving the floor.

"I'm going home with Edith," Sylvia panted.

"You're a strange creature, I've hardly seen you dance a single step," commented the Duchess.

"I...don't feel...well," said Sylvia truthfully.

"Oh, go if you must," said the Duchess. I will inform the Count."

Sylvia kissed the Duchess and Charlotte quickly and hurried to the front door.

The door was wide open and a footman stood at the top of the steps.

Edith's carriage was just drawing away from the kerb.

"Stop!" cried Sylvia, rushing down the steps. Too late! The horses lifted their sprightly legs and the carriage bowled off down the street. The footman regarded Sylvia curiously as she came slowly back up the stairs.

"Did you want your cloak, m'lady?" he asked.

"Thank you, no, I'll be leaving later now."

Sylvia felt she should tell the Duchess that she had not left with Edith after all, but at that moment another waltz struck up. It was no use – the Duchess and Charlotte would be back on the dance floor. She would wait until later. She knew her step-mother was enjoying herself and would not want to leave before midnight.

Sylvia wandered up the wide staircase, seeking somewhere quiet where she could rest unobtrusively. One or two ladies passed her on their way down, their faces bright with freshly applied rouge.

Sylvia pushed open a door and found herself in the boudoir set aside for the ladies as a place to refresh their make-up and hair. There was nobody here but she was sure someone would be up sooner or later. She crossed the boudoir and went through another door. She found herself in a pretty sitting room. A fire was burning merrily in the grate and there was a huge sofa drawn up against the opposite wall.

The sofa looked most inviting.

Sylvia sank onto it thankfully. She curled up and lay down, her head on one of the cushions. It was peaceful and warm here. If she just thought about that...about being so peaceful and warm...perhaps she would manage to forget that icy gaze cast upon her by Lord Robert Farron of Farron Towers...

*

Sylvia stirred and stretched and opened her eyes. A moment later she sat up, alarmed.

The fire in the grate was out and the room was chill. The house seemed as silent as the grave. No music, no voices, no carriage wheels outside.

A huge, blank moon leered in at the window.

Sylvia hurried to the door and opened it. The boudoir was empty. The purses and shawls that had been scattered there earlier were all gone.

The wide staircase was in darkness.

Down the stairs flew Sylvia, feeling like a stowaway on an abandoned ship. She listened in the hallway below for voices. Nothing!

She heard the sound of footsteps approaching and turned just as the footman appeared in the hall. He looked surprised and even suspicious to see Sylvia.

"My lady," he said with a bow.

"W..what time is it?" asked Sylvia nervously.

"It's three o'clock in the morning, my lady. I'm waiting for the last of the guests to depart."

Relief swept over Sylvia. "Oh! There are some people here still?"

"A few gentlemen, my lady. Playing cards. Lady Lambourne has retired."

"All the ladies have left? The Duchess of Belham and…and Lady Charlotte?"

"All departed, my lady."

Sylvia realised that the Duchess and Charlotte had left without her, because she had told them that she was leaving with Edith.

What should she do? She had no wish to disturb Lady Lambourne at this hour.

"Is…the Count von Brauer still here?' she asked at last.

The footman regarded her coolly before replying. "He is, my lady. You will find him in the library."

Sylvia was cold. She asked for her cloak and the footman brought it to her. Then she set off for the library.

The doors were wide open and she heard the murmur of low male voices from the corridor as she approached. She hesitated and then stepped slowly into the fug of smoke and whiskey tainted air.

The Count sat with three other gentlemen. They were

immersed in a game of cards. An empty whiskey bottle stood at the Count's elbow.

Sylvia was about to start forward, when she caught sight of a tall figure lounging at the window.

Lord Farron!

She heartily wished he were not here, but supposed he had felt obliged to remain up with those of his god-mother's guests who had not yet departed.

She stepped forward into the light and was uncomfortably aware of Lord Farron's eyes upon her as she approached the card table.

"C..Count von Brauer. It is I, Sylvia."

The Count's head swung up. "Wha' the devil? I was told you'd gone home with Edith."

"There was a mistake. I was left behind. I would like to go home now."

"Oh, *would* you?" sneered the Count. "Well, I'm doing too well here – "

"Now be a sport," interposed one of the other gentlemen at the table. "Take the little lady home."

"Just 'cos you're losing, Tyndale!" roared the Count. "I won't be – cajoled. D'ye hear? You wait – over there – my girl!

With that, the Count pushed Sylvia towards one of the fireside chairs. She almost fell, but one of the players put out a hand to steady her. Humiliated and helpless, she made her way over to the fireplace and sat down. She stared resolutely into the flames. She would not look at Lord Farron and supposed that he similarly would not look at her.

After a few minutes she was aware of someone leaving the room. She glanced up in time to see Lord Farron passing through the door.

Five minutes later the Count let out a shout of rage and slammed his cards down.

"Dash it, she's brought me bad luck !" he cried. He rose and glowered at Sylvia. "Suppose I might as well take you home, since you've done for me here."

Sylvia rose, trying not to tremble before him. The Count came over and took her elbow roughly. Then, grunting a churlish farewell to the other gentleman, he propelled her from the room.

The footman stood waiting in the hallway.

"You – go fetch me my cloak," cried the Count. The footman hurried off. The Count turned to Sylvia, who shrank from his black gaze.

"I'll teach you – madam – not to ruin a fellow's game. See if I don't," he snorted.

The footman returned with his cloak and the Count flung it over his shoulders.

"I've called up your coach, sir," he said.

"Good, good," said the Count. He fumbled in his waistcoat pocket and handed the footman a coin. Then he pushed Sylvia out of the front door and down the steps.

Neither he nor Sylvia was aware of the figure watching from the dark of the unlit stairway.

This figure now descended the stairs.

"Your coach is waiting outside, sir," said the footman. "Just along the street, as you ordered."

"Thank you," replied Lord Farron simply, before following Sylvia and the Count out into the cold London night.

CHAPTER EIGHT

The Count sat opposite Sylvia in the coach. His head lolled on his shoulders but whenever he raised it to stare at Sylvia, his eyes were baleful.

Sylvia did not know what to say or do. Above even the clatter of the horses' hooves and the rattle of the coach wheels, she could hear the Count's heavy, angry breath.

"I...am sorry you lost at cards, sir. Truly I am," she said at last.

The Count snarled. "A thousand pounds! That's what I lost! A thousand pounds!"

"That is a great deal to lose," admitted Sylvia.

The Count regarded Sylvia for a moment and then shifted forward on his seat so that he was leaning across the space between them.

"How you going to make it up to me? Huh?"

Sylvia sat very still. "H..how do you mean, sir?"

"How do I mean?" The Count smirked and laid a hand on Sylvia's knee. "Why, how do you think I mean, madam?"

Sylvia drew in her breath. The Count was taking inconceivable liberties with her. She pushed his hand away and moved further along the seat. She wondered fleetingly if she had ever been alone with him for even a second in the past...the past that she could not remember. Then she drove the thought from her mind. Her stepmother would never have allowed such a thing, not without a chaperone. It was pure accident that she was alone with him tonight.

It was for this very same reason, that she never for one second imagined there might be a connection between Count Von Brauer and the events of that 'lost' night, when Lord Farron and Charity rescued her. She would never have visited the Count without informing her parents, who would naturally have insisted on a chaperone.

Much as she recoiled from the Count, it never occurred to her that he was a man capable of luring her with falsehoods to his lair.

The Count gave his moustache an almost vicious twist. "The more you refuse me now, the more you'll regret it later!" he growled.

Sylvia remained silent.

The Count, his eyelids drooping, leaned back in his seat. Spittle glistened in his moustache.

Surely it was not possible, thought Sylvia, that she had *ever* been attracted to this man!

She racked her brains to remember some moment of romance or intimacy between them. There was nothing. The Count might as well have been a phantom. If it were not for what he himself had told her – corroborated by her stepmother and her sisters – she would have taken him for an utter stranger.

The wheels of the coach turned with a monotonous rhythm, to which her tortured mind now supplied words.

Going to marry going to marry going to marry…

Sylvia felt movement on her knee and looked down. She found herself regarding her own hand as it nervously picked at the silk of her dress. She quickly laced her gloved fingers together in her lap and turned to look out of the window. She could see a light shining ahead and realised it illumined an attic window of Number One London – the house belonging to the descendants of the Duke of Wellington.

"What are you staring at?" asked the Count. Only one of his eyes was open but it seemed fixed intently on her.

"A…a light. Above the trees. A yellow light. It's shining in the attic of a house by the park there. I think…a maid must be sitting up, darning socks or…something."

Her voice trailed off. The one open eye of the Count glowed like a hot coal in the darkness of the coach. Then suddenly he threw back his head with a roar so loud it made Sylvia start.

"Ha ha ha! Darning socks! Ha ha ha!"

"What is so…comical, sir?"

"You! If a maid is up at this hour it's for more than darning socks. And I wish I was a fly on the wall to see what young blood is – darning with her. Ha ha ha!"

The Count's coarse laughter metamorphosed into a cough. He dragged a handkerchief out of his pocket and spat into it.

Sylvia shrank against the backrest. As she did so she noticed that the faded velvet carried an odour of stale perfume and wax.

"I would hate to think, sir…that a young servant was…being taken advantage of in any way."

"That's what servant girls are for," growled the Count. Registering Sylvia's shock, he waved a hand at her. "Pshaw! What the deuce does a prig like you know about the ways of the world, eh?"

Sylvia felt her face burn. The misery that was engulfing her in this coach seemed but a portend of the misery that stretched ahead. *Going to marry going to marry going to marry.*

"Know what I'm going to do!" exclaimed the Count

suddenly. "I'm going to educate you. Yes! Introduce you to women who are not strangers to the art of *pleasing* a fellow! Knock this priggishness out of you!"

Before Sylvia could utter a word, he thrust his head out of the carriage window and shouted up at the driver.

"To the Black Garter Club. Make haste!"

Sylvia was thrown sideways as the carriage wheeled round and set off back the way they had come.

"I…should like to go home, sir," she gasped. "Take me home!"

"No, my dear, no!" cried the Count. "I want the woman who is to be my wife to be more knowledgeable in the ways of the world!"

The driver whipped the horses on. Sylvia struggled to the window and gazed out, trying to see where they were heading. The handsome houses of Park Lane slipped by…the dark expanse of the park. Then they were hurtling along Oxford Street…the gloomy area around St Giles…plunging on into narrow, ill-lit streets, that even at this hour of the morning were not deserted.

Figures lounged in doorways, men in long cloaks with hoods hiding their faces flitted in and out of carriages and disappeared through lamp-lit doorways. Sylvia was astonished at the sight of such activity, hours after the sun had set and not long before it would rise. Who were these people and did they ever sleep?

The coach drew up outside a wooden, nail-studded door. The Count forced Sylvia out first. Then he gestured to the coachman to wait along the street, by a horse trough. As the coach drew away the Count turned and hammered on the door.

A grille set in the door was drawn aside and a face looked out. It perused the Count and Sylvia for a moment. Then the grille slid shut and a second later the door opened.

A portly doorman, in a striped waistcoat and breeches, beckoned them through. Sylvia hung back, glancing desperately up and down the street as if in the forlorn hope of seeing a friendly face.

The Count squeezed her arm until she almost yelped.

"Come on," he ordered through gritted teeth.

Reluctantly she passed through the nail-studded door with him.

A woman with violent red hair was coming towards them as they entered. She stood aside to allow them to pass.

"Very nice too, Count," she smirked, indicating Sylvia.

Sylvia barely glanced at her as she stumbled on. The passageway was narrow and lit by hissing gas jets. The walls seemed to be covered with posters advertising nightclub acts. There was a musky smell in the air.

The Count kept a grip on Sylvia's elbow to hurry her along.

Down some stairs, covered in surprisingly lush carpet and through a red velvet curtain, Sylvia entered a world she could hardly imagine existed.

Smoke, shot through with the light from several chandeliers, hung in the air like a red mist. The atmosphere was so heavy with various perfumes that Sylvia could barely breathe. Men and women crowded around gaming tables or lounged on sofas. There was the constant sound of champagne corks popping, the buzz of conversation, screeches of triumph or groans of despair as the roulette wheel spun to a halt.

What truly shocked Sylvia, however, was the fact that a great many of the patrons of the establishment seemed to be in various stages of undress.

The men had discarded their cravats…undone their shirt collars…rolled up their sleeves. The women had loosened their hair…were in corsets and bloomers…or dresses cut so low at the front that little was left to the imagination.

Sylvia kept her eyes down as the Count steered her through the jostling, leering crowd.

"She's a ripe one!" leered a large, yellow-faced gentleman, pinching Sylvia's arm.

A woman in bright green with heavily rouged cheeks and dark circles under her eyes, barred their way. Ignoring Sylvia, she reached up and traced a finger over the Count's lips.

"I haven't seen *you* for a few weeks, duckie!" she murmured. "Forgot your little Kitty, have you?"

The Count caught the woman's wrist, turned her hand over, and pressed his lips to her palm. "How could I forget – a woman so talented – in the arts of pleasure?"

Sylvia closed her eyes for a moment. This was a nightmare. The Count was behaving in a reckless manner, as if wishing to provoke his fiancée. She realised that it was the effect of the copious amounts of drink he had no doubt taken that evening and she longed to be out of this place, away from him…safe at home.

What could she do? Was there a single human being here who would help her escape? Whether it was the result of the smoke, or her own fatigue, the faces that loomed about her seemed distorted in feature, garish in colour.

One woman parted full, reddened lips to reveal stumps of black teeth. Another, under clouds of pink powder, betrayed skin marked by smallpox. The eyes of the men seemed inflamed, their cheeks pitted with burst veins.

Sylvia felt plunged into an inferno of vice and depravity.

Other women came to flutter around the Count like floridly coloured birds. Sylvia felt herself elbowed aside.

Then someone slipped an arm under her cloak and round her waist.

It was the yellow-faced gentleman.

"Ah! The little fish has slipped from the net. What bait do I have to use to catch her?"

Sylvia struggled out of his grasp. "N..no bait at all, sir," she stammered. "J..just call me a carriage please and I shall be most obliged."

The yellow-faced gentleman chuckled unpleasantly. "Let the fish go again? Not likely. Why don't we go for a ride in my carriage? There are places I know, secret places, where we'd be undisturbed."

Tears filled Sylvia's eyes. As the gentleman lunged towards her again she drew back, stumbling against the figure of another gentleman behind her.

"I..I'm sorry," she said, without turning.

A firm hand grasped her elbow. "Might I be of service, madam?"

The voice was so wonderfully, reassuringly familiar that Sylvia's head whipped round in immediate relief. "L..Lord Farron. Oh, take me home, please. Take me home!"

She was too faint for the moment to register the utter coldness in his eyes as he bowed in compliance.

"Come with me," he said.

The yellow-faced gentleman stared after them open mouthed.

Lord Farron led Sylvia through the crowd, which parted quickly before him after one glance at his stern, set features.

As they reached the stairway he turned to regard her. "You have everything you came with?" he asked.

Sylvia nodded, now noticing with a pang his cool

manner towards her. As cool as it had been earlier at Lady Lambourne's. Her heart felt as if it would burst. If he had thought so little of her *then*, what must he think of her *now*, having found her at the Black Garter Club?

On the other hand, she thought suddenly, what was Lord Farron himself doing in such a place?

Swallowing, she ventured a question. "H..have you ever…been here before?"

"Never!" he replied curtly.

Puzzled as to why he should then be here on this occasion, she was about to follow Lord Farron up the stairs that led to the exit, when someone caught at her arm and halted her progress.

"What's this? My fiancée sneaking off with a stranger?"

Lord Farron turned from three steps above. "Hardly a stranger, Count von Brauer," he said.

"Ah! It's you, Farron. What's your game?"

"I am taking the young lady home, as she requested," replied Lord Farron coolly.

The Count swayed as he stared at Lord Farron and his words were slurred. "Sheems to be shomething of a habit with you – rescuing damsels – in distress."

Lord Farron's eyes narrowed. "Seems to be something of a habit with you, causing distress," he said. He held his hand out to Sylvia. "Come, madam."

Sylvia was about to take his hand, when the Count burst past her and lunged up the stairs at Lord Farron.

"The devil you'll take Sylvia with you," he grunted.

Lord Farron, stepping to one side, caught hold of the Count's raised arm and hurled him back down the stairs. He landed groaning at Sylvia's feet. His eyes closed and opened and closed again.

He was unconscious.

Sylvia stared down at him. He was her fiancé, but she did not want to touch him or help him. She felt humiliated and embarrassed before Lord Farron.

Lord Farron beckoned to the doorman who had come to the top of the stairs at the sound of the commotion.

"Do you know where this gentleman lodges?" he asked.

"I do," said the doorman. He mentioned the name of a street.

Lord Farron nodded. "Then help me carry him to my coach," he said.

"W..where are you taking him?" asked Sylvia.

Without looking at her, Lord Farron replied. "Since his lodgings lie on the way to Mayfair, I will deposit him there first to – sleep off the effects of this night's entertainments. I will then take you on to your home."

Not saying another word, Sylvia, hanging her head, followed Lord Farron and the doorman as they carried the Count to the coach. Lord Farron gave the address to the coach driver and they set off.

*

Sylvia sat back numbly in the carriage. Neither she nor Lord Farron spoke a word. The Count, sprawled on the seat beside Sylvia, breathed heavily through open lips. Sylvia thought she would die of mortification.

Lord Farron must surely wonder what had drawn her to this odious man in the first place. He must wonder what she had been thinking of, accompanying her fiancé to such a den of iniquity.

Only when the carriage drew to a halt again did Sylvia raise her eyes. For a moment she quite forgot her misery in surprise at what she saw beyond the carriage window.

They did not seem to have travelled far from the Black Garter Club. They were in a mean, gloomy street lined with tall, narrow and grimy houses. Was it possible that the wealthy and well-connected Count lodged in one of these dwellings?

It seemed so, for Lord Farron flung open the door and called for the driver's help in removing the Count.

The Count, however, stirred at this point. Semiconscious, he was able to stagger from the carriage unaided. Lord Farron then put an arm under his shoulder and helped him towards the front door of a house marked number 12. The Count started to fumble in his pockets for a key.

The coach driver settled back in his seat and sat lightly flicking his whip in the cold air.

Sylvia stared at the façade of number 12. Did her father and stepmother know that the Count inhabited such dingy lodgings? Or had the Count been careful to only ever receive guests at his exclusive gentlemen's club in Pall Mall?

A chill ran over her, as she wondered whether it was for its proximity to the Black Garter Club, that the Count had chosen these lodgings in the first place. He certainly must frequent the Black Garter a great deal, to be so familiar with many of its other patrons.

"I need to stretch my legs," said the coachman suddenly above her. He climbed down from his box and strolled off along the street.

Sylvia peered back at the doorway of number 12. The Count seemed to have found his key, for as she looked the front door opened and the two men disappeared inside. The door swung behind them but did not fully close.

She glanced up the street at the retreating figure of the coachman. She realised from the sudden gleam near his mouth that he had lit a cigarette or a pipe. That's what he meant by 'stretch my legs,' she thought wanly.

A man tottered up to the carriage window and looked in.

"My word, but you're a charmer," he mumbled. It was obvious he was drunk.

Sylvia drew back into the darkness of the coach. She had never in her life visited such streets as these nor encountered such people.

The drunk staggered away. Sylvia wrapped her cloak around her. She was beginning to feel cold.

At that moment she heard the sound of a scuffle from within the hallway of number 12.

She flung open the door of the coach and almost tumbled out. She glanced up the street. The coachman was well beyond earshot now. She would have to really shout loudly to attract his attention and who knew what friends of the Count might be lurking nearby? The drunk was clinging to the iron railings of a house further along the street, but she would never have dreamed of approaching him for help.

A cry of rage and then a thud issued from the hallway.

It was clear that the Count had attacked Lord Farron again.

Without another thought Sylvia hurried across the pavement to the Count's lodgings and pushed open the door. She blinked within the shadowy hallway, peering ahead of her.

With a rush of relief she saw the Count lying flat on his back on the cold tiles.

She took a deep breath and then moved down the passageway.

Lord Farron, standing over the Count, looked up at the sound of Sylvia's footsteps.

"He appeared to recover full consciousness and – decided to attack me again," he said. "I'm afraid I had to – knock him out. Rather hard."

Sylvia nodded blankly. She was so thankful that Lord Farron had not been harmed.

A door at the end of the passageway opened and a woman came out. Sylvia recognised the same red-haired woman who had been in the entrance of the Black Garter Club.

"Lor' lummy," the woman said, approaching the recumbent Count, "he's had a skinful, by the looks of it."

"Which is his room?" asked Lord Farron coldly.

The woman raised an eyebrow. "His *suite* is at the top of the house," she replied. "I lit a fire for him when I got in. Need any help getting him up there?"

"None," said Lord Farron. He hoisted the Count on to his shoulders and started up the stairs. Sylvia hesitated and then, under the red-haired woman's amused gaze, followed him up.

Lord Farron kicked open the door to the Count's room.

This was not quite as drab as the rest of the house. Gas flickered in sconces on the wall and a fire burned brightly in the hearth. There were heavy velvet curtains at the window and one or two pieces of fine furniture, including two large sofas. A large book, surrounded by papers and smaller tomes, lay open on a table.

Lord Farron dropped the Count on to one of the sofas and swung his legs up so that he was lying flat. Then he glanced at Sylvia.

"Since you are here, perhaps you had better minister to your – fiancé yourself," he said in a bitter tone.

Sylvia could not look at him. She nodded miserably and then pushed open the door set in the wall opposite. She discovered a washstand and basin in the small bedroom beyond. She poured a little water into the basin and, a flannel over her arm, carried the basin back to the unconscious Count.

Lord Farron observed her from under dark brows all the while. When she undid the Count's collar, however, he turned abruptly away.

Sylvia moistened the flannel in the basin and started to dab the Count's bruised forehead. Her actions were mechanical. She barely registered the Count at all. Although she never fully looked Lord Farron's way, she was yet aware of his every action.

He moved about the room, reading the spines of the books on the shelves, or examining the few paintings on the wall with his head on one side. Sylvia ached for a kind glance or word from him.

There was no sound in the room other than the crackle of the fire and the laboured breathing of the Count.

"I...want you to know...I had no choice but to...accompany the Count...to that dreadful place," said Sylvia at last in a low voice.

Lord Farron straightened a book on the shelf. "I know."

Sylvia was surprised. She moved the Count's hair away from his forehead and started to clean a wound there. "You....you said you had never been...to the club before."

"I haven't."

Sylvia looked up at Lord Farron, perplexed. "Then why....?"

"...was I there tonight?" Lord Farron finished Sylvia's sentence.

Sylvia nodded. Lord Farron seemed to weigh his reply.

"I had reason to believe that I would find – someone there in need of my assistance," he said eventually.

Sylvia flushed at the idea that that someone might be – must surely be – herself. Before she could say a word, however, the Count slipped sideways on the sofa, his head rolling to hang over the edge. Sylvia rushed to support him at the same time as Lord Farron. As they lifted the Count's head back in place, their fingers met.

The touch of Lord Farron's skin on hers sent a jolt through Sylvia. She almost moaned aloud at the sensation.

Lord Farron himself stepped back as if burnt by the encounter. He passed a hand across his brow and then stared down at the Count. His lip curled in distaste.

"Why are you to give yourself – to that man?" he burst out fiercely.

Sylvia flushed again but did not – could not – reply. Lord Farron turned on his heel and continued his prowl of the room.

She dipped the flannel into the basin again and dabbed away a trickle of blood that had run down the Count's cheek. Every so often she cast an agonised gaze at Lord Farron.

Lord Farron halted before the table on which was spread open the large, leather-bound tome. Lord Farron started as he saw that this was an ancient book of astronomy. In the middle of the open pages, a paper weight held down a piece of red-stained cloth. Leaning close to look, Lord Farron gave a loud exclamation.

Sylvia looked at him, the flannel held in mid-air. She did not notice water starting to drip on the Count's face.

"W..what is it?" she ventured to ask.

Lord Farron frowned at her. "I'm not sure," he said.

The cloth appeared to be a square of bandage and the red on it was – blood. The pages that lay beneath depicted a section of the sky at night, with all the stars marked.

He took up the cloth. There was writing on it in black ink and, holding it closer to a gas lamp that stood on the table, he began to read.

It was at this point that the Count, perhaps half drawn to consciousness by the drops of water on his face, began to mutter insensibly.

Sylvia turned and stared down at him.

"*Below the one and then below – the greater O – cannot but follow – alpha's light – within the maze – holy stone –* "

Sylvia frowned. His words made no sense to her.

Lord Farron, at first deeply engrossed in reading the cloth, suddenly looked up and listened with a keener ear to the Count's delirious words. He looked back at the cloth.

"He is repeating some of what is written here," he said slowly.

"And w..what is that?" asked Sylvia in a low voice.

"It appears to be a poem or riddle of some kind," responded Lord Farron. "It corresponds in some way to the – map of the heavens – open on this page."

"That book belongs to the Count?" asked Sylvia in disbelief. Her fiancé had never mentioned an interest in astronomy to her.

"Let me see," said Lord Farron. With his free hand he flicked the pages to the frontispiece of the book. A name was written there on a bookplate.

"*Chagnon*" he read aloud.

At the sound of this name the Count suddenly became agitated. He started to flail about and his mutterings grew louder. Sylvia drew away from him and turned eyes of dismay towards Lord Farron.

"There is an address here too," continued Lord Farron. "*20 Rue de Vieux Tolbiac, Paris.*"

"Paris!" echoed Sylvia. She did not remember the Count ever mentioning a sojourn in Paris. What else was she to discover about her fiancé? She stared down at him, lying there beneath her, his moustache damp with a mixture of water and blood, his thin red lips parted to reveal small white teeth, his arms dangling at his side.

One day those thin lips must meet hers…those arms must enfold her! The idea of such contact with him struck her like a blow. She let fall the flannel and pressed her palms to her eyes.

She suddenly felt so tired, so defeated. Her legs began to buckle under her.

"Can we…go now?" she asked tremblingly.

Lord Farron did not reply. He stood examining the cloth. He read what was written there again, a frown on his features. Then he turned the cloth over and his frown deepened.

On the other side, written in blood, was a single word, which he murmured aloud in surprise.

"*Belham.*"

CHAPTER NINE

Jeannie gave a light tap on Sylvia's door and entered without summons. The young mistress was probably still fast asleep, the maid thought. She had arrived home so late last night, well after the Duchess. The whole house had been locked and bolted, as if the Duchess wasn't expecting her step-daughter home at all.

It was lucky that Jeannie was up and about. It was her first time in London and she was finding it hard to sleep at night with the excitement.

She was in the kitchen making herself some hot tea when she'd heard a carriage draw up outside and someone with a light footfall get out and cross the pavement. She'd gone out on the front steps – in her night-robe and shawl, what would they say back at the castle! – and there was Lady Sylvia, just about to ring the bell.

Lady Sylvia was that tired and pale – and that pleased to see Jeannie – she'd burst into tears right there on the steps. The carriage that had brought her home started off and poor Lady Sylvia, she'd given such a longing look after it, Jeannie thought it must be her fiancé driving away. Jeannie wondered if they'd had a quarrel.

She hummed quietly to herself now, as she deposited the breakfast tray she was carrying on to the table at the foot of the bed and went over to open the curtains. Most of the staff in the London house had been dismissed when the family left for Castle Belham and she was having to undertake duties that would not normally be her lot. But she didn't mind one bit. It made life all the more interesting.

She turned back to the tray and gave a start.

"You're awake, my lady."

Sylvia was already sitting up in bed, wrapped in a pale blue shawl. Her gaze slid by Jeannie and settled on the grey square of sky on the other side of the window.

"Yes, I'm awake."

"Well, there's some lovely fresh rolls here, and damson jam. The jam's from Belham. I brought a few jars with me in a basket. I thought to myself, they won't get jam as good as this in London, so they won't. Shall I butter the rolls for you?"

Without answering, Sylvia threw back the bedclothes and felt for her slippers.

Jeannie stood poised with the butter knife. "Is there something else I can get for you, my lady?"

"No, thank you, Jeannie. I don't want any breakfast. Thank you."

Jeannie was left speechless as Sylvia flung on a dressing gown and hurriedly left the room.

"Well!" she said after a moment. She looked at the butter on the end of the knife and, thinking *waste not want not*, licked it cleanly off the blade herself.

Sylvia hurried along the corridor, her mind in turmoil.

She had felt so faint those last few minutes at the Count's lodgings that she had barely registered Lord Farron reading the name *BELHAM* on the cloth. She had barely registered him copying the words from the cloth onto a piece of paper, which he then folded and put into his waistcoat. She dimly remembered that they had left the Count comatose but comfortable on the couch – she had done as much as duty demanded – and had descended the unlit stairway together.

Lord Farron had not taken her hand to guide her and she had been glad of that, yes, glad, for his touch was so like a fiery brand on her skin, she might have cried out.

Lord Farron had not spoken as he brought Sylvia home. When at last they drew up outside the Belham house he had merely inclined his head in acknowledgement at her "good-night and…thank you."

His mind – his heart – had seemed elsewhere.

He had become as distant to her as the stars in the sky.

Sylvia reached her step-mother's boudoir and stood outside the door for a moment, her heart hammering. Then she lifted her hand and knocked. There was a sleepy moan from within and Sylvia pushed the door open.

The Duchess was in a semi-recumbent position, propped up with pillows. She did not like to sleep flat on her back as this meant her mouth fell open during the night and *noxious vapours* might get in. Never mind the odd insect.

Sylvia crossed to the end of the bed.

"Mama?"

The Duchess lifted an eyelid and closed it again with a low groan.

"Mama! Please wake up. I have something to tell you." Sylvia waited patiently for a moment and then went on. "Mama, listen. I cannot marry the Count."

Two eyelids flew open at this. "What? What was that?"

Sylvia did not falter. "I cannot marry the Count."

The Duchess struggled to an upright position, clutching at the canopy around the bed for support.

"What am I hearing? What nonsense is this?"

"The nonsense, Mama, is for you to expect me to marry a man I detest and despise."

The Duchess clasped her breast in dismay. "Oh! It is

too early in the morning to distress me so. How can you say such things about a man you barely know?"

"That is exactly it," said Sylvia as patiently as she could. "I barely know him. None of us knows him. If you had been with me last night...'

"Last night?" shrieked the Duchess. "Last night you hardly spent a minute with him. You went home early with your sister."

"I did not go home with my sister. There was a mistake and I was left behind. I found myself much later having recourse to the...protection of the Count. He took me to...a place that no lady of repute should ever be taken to. No true gentleman could ever behave in the way he did. He was drunk, mama, drunk!"

The Duchess was listening in alarm. She could see the promised improvement in the Belham family fortunes vanish like a mist.

"Drunk? Pooh!" she cried. "You will have to get used to that in men, my girl. Even your father has had to be carried home from his club on one or two occasions. The Count no doubt is getting nervous about the forthcoming marriage. After all, you hardly encourage him with your behaviour. You betray no affection for him whatsoever."

"That is because I *feel* no affection!" said Sylvia with steely calm. "His behaviour to me last night was insulting in the extreme. If it had not been for the intercession of Lord Farron, I do not know what would have happened to me."

At the sound of that name, the Duchess almost leapt from the bed in fury. "Ah! Now I understand! This is nothing to do with the behaviour of the Count and everything to do with the behaviour of Lord Farron. He had the impertinence to call here one afternoon asking for you but I soon sent him packing."

Sylvia stared at her stepmother. She remembered the

day Lord Farron had called at the house and not even been admitted.

"W..what did you say to him?" she asked in as calm a tone as she could muster.

"I *said* nothing, my dear. I had one of the servants take him a note explaining that you were indisposed and would remain so as far as he was concerned."

Sylvia tried to keep her voice steady. "Was it clear the note...was from you?"

The Duchess for the first time looked a little uncomfortable.

"He may have been – led to believe – that it was from *you.*"

Sylvia was beginning to feel faint. "From...from me?"

The Duchess drew herself up quickly. "I did what I believed was the best thing in the circumstances. I could not allow you to be distracted by this young man."

Sylvia felt for the arm of a chair and sat down. Now she understood why Lord Farron had grown so cold towards her. He had every reason to believe she had grown cold towards *him.*

"You had...no right to do that," she said tremblingly.

"No right? I had every right. I was protecting the interests of my family. And what is more I was protecting *you.* And I will go on protecting you. You have got some silly notion into your head about the Count, comparing him unfavourably to this – Lord Farron – a man who doesn't even own a full set of Chippendale! You have made your promise to the Count and you will keep that promise. Everything depends on it."

Sylvia rose to her feet in a daze. "I see I must go to Papa."

The Duchess threw up her hands. "Oh, do, go to him,

why don't you! Distress him, why don't you! He's only recovering from the prospect of bankruptcy and death. He'll welcome your change of mind with open arms, I'm sure."

"He would never wish me to be unhappy," said Sylvia, moving towards the door.

"Happiness!" shrieked the Duchess. "Happiness is for puppies and – and parrots! It is most certainly not for married women!"

As Sylvia closed the boudoir door behind her, she heard the Duchess ringing furiously for her maid.

*

Tompkins was astonished to open the door of the Belham coach and see only Sylvia preparing to descend.

"You are alone, my lady?" he asked, peering beyond her into the coach, as if the Duchess might at any moment pop up from under the cushions.

Sylvia took his hand and stepped down from the coach. "Yes, Tompkins, I am."

"Oh," said Tompkins. "Only when the message came asking for the train to be met, I thought you were both coming home."

"No. Only myself."

"Well, you're right welcome, my lady. The Duke is looking forward to seeing you."

"How is my father?"

"So much better, my lady. You'd hardly believe it."

Sylvia felt a surge of relief. "I'll go straight up and see him," she said.

The door to her father's room was ajar. She stood there for a moment, looking in.

Her father was sitting up in bed. Across the counterpane were strewn various papers, one of which he was examining through a magnifying glass. He looked up with delight when he heard Sylvia's gentle "Papa!"

"My dear! Come, come sit here on the bed. Oh, how I've missed you and your mama!"

Sylvia sat on the edge of the bed, scanning her father's face as she did so. Colour had returned to his cheek and his eyes were lively again.

"You must tell me all about London!" he said. "How's the house? I'm not going to have to sell it now, you know. Your mama can keep all her treasures – keep up her society life. All thanks to the Count."

Sylvia drew in her breath. "Ah, yes. The Count. Papa, I want to…"

"You're marrying a generous fellow, my dear."

"Generous, maybe, but..."

"He's said he'll even pay for us to keep the Riveria property.'

This was the first Sylvia had heard of this and her heart started to sink. The more the Count offered, the more was lost by her decision not to marry him.

Her father went happily on. "I'm happy enough just keeping Belham, as you know. The Count has said I am absolutely to return here to live, once all the repairs are effected."

"The repairs, yes," murmured Sylvia.

"You and he, of course, will be off then to his estates in Bavaria." The Duke turned down the corners of his mouth. "Can't say as I shall like that much. Bavaria might as well be the Orient. Too far for my old bones to travel, eh?"

"Too far," echoed Sylvia.

She should speak. Now, before this conversation went too far. She should speak.

"Papa," she began, reaching for his hand. "I have

something to tell you."

"Have you, my dear? About your trousseau, I'll be bound. But look – just look here. Just one second. Do you know what these papers are? They're blueprints, plans! The Count – oh, you've got a prize there, you have – he told me to set about organising what needs to be done here. I went around on Tompkins' arm – now don't look at me like that! I only did an hour here, an hour there – but I saw enough. I found the original floor plans in the archives, would you believe! I've been able to work from those."

The Duke's eyes were flashing with pleasure. He was more animated than Sylvia had seen him for a long time. He was not slurring his words and his hand was steady. He was better, yes, better. *Because his life was better*. Because his beloved Castle Belham was to be saved, because his beloved family name was not after all to fall into disrepute. He was not going to be made a penniless bankrupt.

Slowly, Sylvia drew away her hand from his.

It was her sacrifice that had wrought this miracle. How could she now take away what she had given?

"I must…go to my room, Papa," she said, rising to her feet.

"What? Oh, of course. You must be exhausted."

Sylvia nodded absently. The Duke now put down his magnifying glass and gazed at her, just for a moment distracted from his new found pleasure.

"You – fighting fit, my girl?"

"Fighting fit, papa."

"And – happy?"

Sylvia lifted her head. There was a long pause and then at last she gave a nod.

"Yes, Papa," she said.

Happy!

*

The next morning, after a somewhat sleepless night, Sylvia went down to the stables to see Columbine.

Columbine thrust her brown head over the top of her stall and whinnied with pleasure.

When the Duchess had so hurriedly fetched her step-daughter away from Farron Towers, poor Columbine had been left behind. Since Sylvia and the Duchess left for London the very next day, it had been over a fortnight since Columbine had seen her young mistress.

Sylvia stood stroking the horse's velvety nose.

"Who brought her from Farron Towers?" she asked the stable boy.

The boy was sweeping out Columbine's stall and stopped to lean on the broom, which was almost as tall as he.

"The gentlemen hisself."

"Lord Farron?"

"That's right. He rode his own horse and led Columbine on. There was roses on her head."

Sylvia creased her brow. "What do you mean?"

"Tucked into her halter. Pink roses. I put them in a jar over there. See?"

Sylvia turned. There by the stable door was a cracked jar containing a bunch of faded flowers. The roses Lord Farron had sent to her in her room at Farron Towers.

"They're dead," she said sadly.

"That's right, miss. Dead as jackdaws."

Sylvia gave a wan smile. She knew the boy had been shooting at jackdaws, as they had been killing some of the smaller birds in the woods.

The stable boy resumed his sweeping.

Sylvia went slowly back towards the castle. She raised her head as she heard a commotion at the front entrance. The Belham coach stood there, the horses steaming, Tompkins and Jeannie and a couple of other servants hauling packages from the rack.

The Duchess was issuing orders, one hand clamped to the top of her hat to keep it on in the fresh breeze. When she saw Sylvia she gave a squawk and hurried over to her. She came to within an inch of Sylvia and fixed her with her green, enquiring eyes.

"Well?" she said meaningfully.

Sylvia stared at her step-mother. "What do you mean by 'well', mama?"

The green eyes were screwed up until they were the size of peas. "IS IT ON OR IS IT OFF?"

Sylvia had known perfectly well what it was her step-mother wanted to know. Now she felt her teeth clench behind her lips, as she replied. "It..is…on."

The Duchess beamed. "I knew you'd see sense! I've brought your whole trousseau down. A step-mother's intuition!"

She bustled back to the entrance steps where the heap of parcels, hatboxes, and trunks retrieved from the coach was growing by the minute.

Sylvia followed. She stepped around the pile and into the castle, where she went up to her room and lay on her chaise longue. She felt numb with misery. Since she had arrived home yesterday and seen her father, she had barely lifted a finger to do anything.

She had, however, managed one constructive task since her return. She had sent a letter to Charity Farron. She wanted Charity to know that it was not *she,* Sylvia, who had turned Lord Farron from their London house, but the Duchess.

Let Lord Farron and Charity think anything of her but that she had spurned their friendship.

That afternoon Jeannie knocked breathlessly on

Sylvia's door.

"It's your fiancé, my lady. He's paid a call."

Sylvia rose reluctantly and descended to the drawing room.

She had not heard from the Count since the evening of the Black Garter Club. She had imagined he would wait a day or two longer, like a fox outside a coop, to see what Sylvia would do. Yet here he was!

She stood at the entrance to the drawing room looking in. The Count was pacing the floor in a state of some agitation. He suddenly stopped and wheeled round as if sensing her presence.

Their eyes locked and Sylvia was startled to see as much dislike in his gaze as she imagined was evident in hers.

"No doubt you are expecting an apology?" hissed the Count.

"I do not believe, sir, that it is…within your nature."

"Ha! You think you know me so well, do you?" jeered the Count.

Sylvia bent her head in silence.

The Count stared at her, chewing his moustache nervously. "So how much – did you tell your step-mother?"

Sylvia raised her head. "Do you think that if I had told my step-mother anything at all of what happened, you would have been admitted to Castle Belham this morning?"

The Count shrugged. "I think I'd be admitted as long as the Duchess wanted new curtains and a box at the opera."

Sylvia flinched. "You are, sir, a man with neither principles nor courtesy."

"But you are still going to marry me, yes?" sneered the Count.

Sylvia bit her lip. "Yes," she said in a small voice.

She thought that her reply would lessen the Count's

137

agitation but to her surprise it did not. He stood biting the inside of his thumb – another habit, thought Sylvia, that she would have to accustom herself to. He obviously had something else he wished to confront his fiancée with, but before he had made his mind up to speak Sylvia heard the Duchess's voice behind her.

"Count von Brauer! How delightful to see you."

Hand extended to greet the Count, the Duchess swooped by Sylvia.

The Count bent over the Duchess's hand, murmuring pleasantries that Sylvia suspected were mere artifice.

The Duchess had no such suspicions and seemed positively skittish with the Count. "What a naughty man you are, leaving it till now to come to see us! Why, Sylvia's been home two days! I'm not going to monopolise your attention, never fear. I'm sure you have much to discuss!"

With this, the Duchess retired to her wing chair where a book lay open on a cushion. Sitting there, she was turned away from the room and was to all intents and purposes unable to see the engaged couple.

The Count indicated to Sylvia that they should draw to one side. Without a word, she followed him across to the window where they sat together on the window seat. Sylvia endeavoured to move even her skirt away from his person. She wished no part of her body or attire to touch his.

The Count crossed a leg over his knee and drummed his fingers on his thigh, his eyes fixed on the chair where the Duchess sat.

"I regret you did not appreciate my attempt to add spice to your dreary existence," he muttered at last.

"I should never appreciate such…spice, as you call it. Neither now nor when we are…married."

"*When we are married –* " repeated the Count, with a strange growl.

Sylvia closed her eyes, as if to shut out the sight of his thin, leering lips and vicious gaze. She opened them again quickly, as she felt the Count lift her chin and turn her face toward him.

"You were not alone with me in my lodgings," he hissed.

"N..no," she admitted.

"It will be the worse for Lord Farron if I catch him in your company again."

"That is unlikely," said Sylvia bitterly.

"What did you see there?"

"W..where?"

"In Cutler Street."

"C..Cutler Street?"

"Damn you!" The Count pinched Sylvia's flesh tight. "My lodgings. Something is missing. What did you – or he – find there?"

"NOTHING!" shouted Sylvia, so loudly that the Duchess shifted in her chair and looked round. The Count immediately released Sylvia from his grip.

"Did you call me, dear?" the Duchess asked Sylvia.

"No, Mama," said Sylvia as calmly as she could.

"Oh," said the Duchess. "Well, I will order tea in a moment. As soon as I've finished this chapter." She took up her book again and turned away from the window.

Sylvia blinked away tears. The Count had hurt her. The lower part of her face actually felt bruised. She did not know the significance of the astronomy book nor the riddle written on the piece of cloth that had so interested Lord Farron, but of one thing she was sure. She would not reveal anything to the Count of what Lord Farron had said or done or found, beyond the obvious.

"Lord Farron carried you to your room after you

had…attacked him. I bathed your injuries. That is all there is to tell," said Sylvia stoutly.

The Count sprung to his feet and looked down at his fiancée, biting his thumb again.

"Even if he has it," he muttered, almost to himself, "what good will it do him, eh? It will do him no good at all. Why? Because he lacks the final key. He lacks – ha ha ha – he lacks Lady Sylvia. Yes. You're the prize, my dear."

"*Prize*?" repeated Sylvia. "I…the *prize*?"

"Oh, you are, my beauty, you are. But let all this deuced waiting be over. Let me have you – ha ha – in my bed, in my possession – no more of these tedious conventions."

Sylvia felt chilled.

Why was the Count so eager to marry her when he was patently less than enchanted by her, and she by him? Or was it perhaps that last fact that lured him on – the challenge of breaking her will, her heart?

The Count spun round as the Duchess said something from her seat by the fire.

"What?" he growled.

The Duchess's head appeared around the side of the wing chair. "I said, what a satisfying conclusion?"

"To what, madam?"

"Why, to this." The Duchess held up the book. "After many vicissitudes – mistaken identity – kidnap – murder – earthquakes – after many delays, the young lovers are finally united!"

She rose magisterially and beamed at the Count and Sylvia.

"Don't give me vicissitudes!" cried the Count. "Don't give me delays. I've had enough! Let's get this wedding over and done with."

The Duchess was taken aback. "Well of course, we are all anxious to – "

"Not anxious enough," snarled the Count. He took up his whip from where he had left it on a side table. "Let's set it for the end of this week."

The Duchess cast a frantic eye at Sylvia. "The end of – but that's two weeks earlier than planned,"

"The end of this week or forget it," snapped the Count.

Sylvia clasped her hands before her, taking an almost grim satisfaction at the sight of the Duchess almost lost for words.

Her step-mother was at last catching a glimpse of Count Von Brauer's other face!

"Which day do you mean exactly?" spluttered the Duchess, coming closer.

The Count raised his whip and appeared to trace extravagant letters in the air.

"Do you read that?" he asked.

The Duchess stared into the air. "I'm not sure I – followed."

"I'LL DO IT AGAIN," scowled the Count.

This time the Duchess diligently followed each flourish of the whip with her eye.

"F – R – I – D – A – Y?" she ventured.

"Bravo!" The Count bowed, first to Sylvia, then to the Duchess. "How simple it all is when you decide. Friday, then. I leave the rest of the details to you."

With that, thrusting his whip under his arm, the Count strode from the room.

"Well I never," murmured the Duchess. "He must be head over heels in love, my dear."

Sylvia did not reply. Her gaze was fixed at the point

in the air where the Count had spelled out that suddenly ominous word. She could almost see the letters hovering there, dark and threatening silhouettes.

Friday. The day when her fate would be sealed forever.

*

Sylvia stood patiently in her wedding dress while the dress-maker teased out the folds of white satin that made up the train.

"Beautiful," breathed the Duchess,

"If I say so myself, Your Grace," simpered the dress-maker, "it's a gorgeous dress and it was no trouble at all to take it in."

"Well, you didn't have to take it in by much!" said the Duchess with a toss of her head.

"Oh, not by the width of a mouse-tail," said the dress-maker quickly.

The Duchess, not sure if she was being made fun of, stared hard at the dress-maker, who bent to her task with redoubled interest. She was shortening the train as the Duchess thought it would look too long in the small chapel where the marriage would take place. It had been appropriate for her when she married the Duke because *their* wedding had taken place in a cathedral.

"Do you wish the train to be shortened by three feet or four?" the Duchess asked Sylvia.

"I leave the decision to you, mama," said Sylvia wearily. She had not even looked at her reflection in the pier glass.

"Four!" the Duchess commanded the dress-maker.

A few more pins were put in place and then Sylvia was allowed to slip out of the dress.

It was indeed a beautiful dress, thought Sylvia, but to

her it might as well have been a shroud.

She excused herself and said she wanted some fresh air.

As she stepped out of the castle she saw a figure with a parasol approach through the trees.

Her heart began to pound as she recognised the figure to be that of Charity Farron!

Charity stopped a foot or so away. The two women stood facing each other in silence for a few moments. Then Charity smiled and held out a hand.

"Oh, it is so good to see you!" exclaimed Sylvia, rushing to clasp her friend's hand. "But where is your carriage?"

"I left it at the gates and walked. The air is so fresh and fragrant. Besides, I was not sure of a general welcome, so I did not wish to advertise my arrival. I was hoping I would be able to get a message to you."

Sylvia looked bewildered. "Not sure of a welcome?"

"Your step-mother would associate me with my brother, and she turned *him* away from your London house. You told me so yourself in your recent letter."

Sylvia blushed. "Oh, yes, I was so ashamed...of her behaviour...when I found out."

"Don't be," said Charity. "She meant it for the best. She was – afraid of your friendship with my brother."

Sylvia was not sure what Charity meant by this, but she was glad that it was Charity and not she who had introduced the topic of Lord Farron.

"H..how is Lord Farron?" she asked eagerly.

Charity stood tracing lines in the dust with the tip of her parasol. "He is well. He has gone away."

Although Sylvia had harboured no hopes of seeing Lord Farron again, this news struck like a fist at her breast.

"G..gone away?"

"Yes. To Paris. On business."

Sylvia heard the word 'Paris' and frowned. She had heard that city mentioned so recently, but where? Before she could dwell any further on the subject, however, Charity took her arm.

"Come, you must tell me all your news. You are to be married at the end of June, I believe?"

"The end of June? Oh, no," said Sylvia, her voice trembling. "It is to be sooner than that. I am to be married the day after tomorrow. Friday."

Charity stood stock still. "Friday?"

"Yes."

"That is – very soon."

Sylvia nodded slowly. "Yes. It is. But I hope, now that we are so happily re-acquainted, you will come to my wedding. It is to be very modest. It was decided that the castle is in too poor a state for a grand wedding breakfast…and then my…fiancé decided he wished the date to be brought forward, so there was no time to find another venue…it's all been rather rushed. But you will come, won't you? Say yes. I would so like there to be someone there who…understood me a little…please come, Charity."

Charity raised her head and Sylvia was taken aback when she saw her friend's face.

Charity's soft, brown eyes were full of tears.

"Yes, Sylvia," she said quietly. "I will come."

Even as she said these words, the tears spilled over and ran in two glistening rivulets down her cheeks.

"It should be me who is weeping," said Sylvia in wonder. "It should be me!"

CHAPTER TEN

The wedding was over and the guests had assembled in the drawing room to take champagne.

It was a small gathering. Apart from the Duke and Duchess, and of course the Count, there was the Count's Best Man, a club acquaintance called Braider, and Charity. Edith and Charlotte were also present, but the sudden change of the wedding date meant their husbands, both away on business, had not returned in time to join them.

Sylvia, pale and silent, had gone upstairs to change her dress.

The Count drank five glasses of champagne and then called for more.

A different servant returned with the tray. When the Duchess saw who it was, her hand flew to her breast. The Count had said he would send someone from his own household to help out at the castle today, but the Duchess had not expected to see *Polly*.

"What are *you* doing here, girl?" she asked bluntly.

"I work for the Count," said Polly, sticking her chin out.

"Is there a problem?" asked the Count, turning.

"I – really would rather not have this girl working here," replied the Duchess.

The Count narrowed his eyes. "He who pays the piper

calls the tune, madam," he said.

The Duchess was too stunned to reply.

After the wedding breakfast the guests returned to the drawing room.

The Count smoked cigars and talked loudly. The Duke dozed in his chair. Sylvia noticed that Charity kept throwing glances at the large grandfather clock that stood in the corner.

"Surely…you do not wish to leave…so soon?" she asked sadly.

Charity pressed her hand. "No, of course not."

Sylvia gave a pale smile and wandered over to the window. Rain teemed down the panes and outside it was dark as a tomb.

"Madam," said the Count's voice in her ear, "why won't you join the company?"

"I do not care to," responded Sylvia, without turning.

The Count leaned in closer. Sylvia could feel his breath stir the curls on her neck.

"The hour is near when I will teach you what it is to be a wife," he hissed.

"But until that hour, please leave me be!" Sylvia replied in a low voice.

She was distracted by the reflection in the mirror of someone entering the room with a tray of coffee. The figure seemed familiar to Sylvia but for a moment she could not place her. She turned to look.

It was Polly.

Sylvia remembered that Polly had run away from Castle Belham, but she did not remember at that moment anything else about her.

Polly advanced toward Sylvia and the Count.

"Coffee, sir?" she asked.

146

"Why, Polly, you should offer it to my – *wife* first."

Polly made a face. "All right," she said sullenly. "Coffee, your – *ladyship*?." Sylvia shook her head. She passed a hand over her forehead.

"What...what are you doing here, Polly?" she asked.

Polly grunted with annoyance. "Why do people keep asking me that? I'm here because I work for him." She pointed at the Count.

The Count grinned. "That's enough now, Polly, you naughty girl," he said.

Sylvia's heart seemed to suddenly miss a beat.

That's enough now, Polly, you naughty girl.

Why did these words sound so familiar to her?

Polly sauntered off with the tray. The Count moved away with his cup and saucer.

Blood was beating loudly in Sylvia's ears.

That's enough now, Polly, you naughty girl.

She had heard it, spoken in just that way, somewhere else. Where?

An image began to form. A room with red walls...an unlit fire...then she saw herself following Polly down some stairs. The Count on a sofa...Polly leaning down to place coffee before him and before Sylvia...*you won't have need of a fire, not with his lordship there*...the Count laughing, yes, laughing...*that's enough now, Polly, you naughty girl*...

And then! And then! Sylvia felt blood drain from her face, as she remembered at last what had followed those words on that fateful night at Endecott... Her pulse raced and her heart thumped against her ribs. She sank, near fainting, onto the window seat. She could not breathe!

"Sylvia, are you all right?"

Charity hovered anxiously before her.

"I remember, Charity. I remember. That night...when

147

you encountered me on the road…I remember."

Charity went pale. It was clear that the returning memory brought not relief, but further torment.

"What happened?" she asked in a low voice.

Sylvia opened her mouth to speak and then froze.

What was the use? It was too late. To divulge what she now knew would only cause distress to her family, impede her father's recovery. And what after all could the truth alter now? It was too late. She was married!

Sylvia shook her head and turned away. "Nothing. I…got lost in the storm, as we all supposed."

Charity narrowed her eyes but said nothing. Her gaze moved beyond her friend to the dark, rainy night outside.

She appeared to scan the darkness as if looking for someone, something. When nothing revealed itself, she dropped her hand and turned away.

The Count had noticed Charity at the window with Sylvia and frowned to himself. He now weaved his way across the room and confronted his wife.

"What did that woman have to say to you, eh?"

"Nothing, nothing."

"It is always 'nothing' with you," mimicked the Count. He tugged at his moustache and then suddenly made up his mind.

"Come, madam," he said, holding out his hand with a leer. "Let us retire now."

Sylvia shrank in horror against the window, the cold pane pressing at her back.

Now that she knew the full extent of the Count's dastardliness, her courage was failing her.

The Count's countenance darkened. "You must – obey me now," he said threateningly.

It took all Sylvia's courage to rise, trembling, to her

feet.

"Good-night everybody," he said to the company en route to the door. "We are…about to retire."

Edith and Charlotte began to clap. The Duchess bit her lip for a moment and then joined in. The Duke followed suit. Soon everyone was participating in the applause except Charity, whose face had crumpled in dismay at the Count's announcement.

The Count's grip tightened on her in the hallway as he sensed Sylvia dragging her feet. When she stumbled on the stairway he pulled at her angrily.

"Come on! Come on!"

Sylvia put one foot before another in almost mechanical fashion.

It was the Count who opened the double doors of the room that had been prepared as a bridal suite and thrust Sylvia through.

Once inside he let go of Sylvia and started to undo his cravat. He flung it off into a corner and then staggered off to the dressing room.

"Be ready – when I return," he called over his shoulder.

As Sylvia was wondering where Jeannie was – Jeannie had been assigned to be her lady's maid tonight – there came a soft tap at the door.

"Come in," said Sylvia, flooded with relief at the thought of a friendly face.

But it was a grinning Polly who entered.

"W..where's Jeannie?" asked Sylvia in dismay.

"I let fall a tray and all the glasses broke and Jeannie cut her finger picking up the pieces and so she sent *me* up while she was getting it seen to." Polly spoke at careless speed, her eyes wandering all over the room and never settling on Sylvia.

Sylvia said nothing in reply, only indicated that Polly unhook her dress for her.

Polly hummed to herself as she helped Sylvia out of her dress and into the shift, after which Sylvia went to sit at the dressing table.

"Please unpin my hair," said Sylvia.

Still humming, Polly came over and started to roughly pull out the pins that held up Sylvia's hair, until it fell in a golden mass on to her shoulders.

Sylvia picked up a brush and then turned her head, as there came the distant sound of pounding at the front door below.

"Someone's carriage has just arrived," commented Polly with a shrug.

Sylvia turned back to the mirror. Her face was pale as alabaster. As the memory of that night at Endecott flooded her mind again, she thought of what it portended for the night to come. With a small cry she dropped the brush and covered her face with her hands.

Polly seemed not to hear. She had wandered towards the doors and opened them. "There's a bit of a ruction going on down below. I'm going to see!"

Sylvia raised her face from her hands. As the double doors closed behind Polly the dressing room door opened and the Count emerged, in a royal blue dressing gown.

He padded over to Sylvia and stood behind her, gazing at her in the mirror.

"This is a distraction," he mused, almost as if she were not there, "but none the less pleasurable for all that." He was so preoccupied he seemed not to hear the loud voices issuing from below. With a sudden move he grasped Sylvia's hair in his hand and leaned over with a leer to kiss her lips.

There was the sound of feet pounding up the stairs –

voices of alarm – and the double doors burst open.

"Unhand her, sir!" came a fierce and commanding voice.

Sylvia almost cried out with joy to see, in the mirror, the figure of Lord Farron advancing on the Count.

Behind him, in the doorway, loomed the bewildered faces of her family and the wedding guests.

The Count swung round with a curse. "What the deuce – how dare you, sir, enter my room like this!"

"Thank God I am not too late!" cried Lord Farron, as his eyes settled on the trembling form of Sylvia at the dressing table.

"Too – late, sir!" spluttered the Count. Too late for what?"

"Too late to prevent a terrible injustice!" proclaimed Lord Farron grimly.

"What injustice? What is going on?" asked the Duke, hobbling forward on the arm of Edith.

"I do not know what the fool is talking about," snarled the Count, "but he will answer for this outrage."

"And you will answer for an even greater outrage!" cried Lord Farron. "Perhaps you would care to explain to the assembled company *why* you married Lady Sylvia when you were *not in a position to do so*?"

The Count blenched but quickly recovered himself. He gave a wild laugh. "You are mad! You have concocted some fairy tale in order to prevent the – the consummation of my marriage."

In the shocked silence that followed, a voice was heard murmuring softly from the doorway.

"So I am a fairy tale, monsieur?"

The company gasped – the Count turned white as death – as a woman with a veil over her face glided into the room.

"Who is this lady?" asked the Duke in bewilderment.

Lord Farron took the woman's hand and bowed to the Duke.

"Your Grace," he said, "allow me to present Helen Chagnon Brauer, wife to the present Count von Brauer of Bavaria."

For a second no-one moved. Then all eyes turned in horror to the Count.

"Damn you, Farron, damn you," he snarled, his lips drawn back from his teeth.

"No, damn *you* ,sir," said the Duke brokenly. "You will be brought to justice for this!"

"Never!" cried the Count.

Sylvia's hand flew to her mouth as the Count rushed to the half open window that led on to the balcony and dived through. She saw him hesitate for a second on the balcony balustrade and then, as Lord Farron and Braider raced to reach him, he leaped wildly out into the air.

"No!" cried Sylvia and Charity as Lord Farron vaulted onto the balustrade to follow him.

"Good God, sir," said the Duke. "Don't attempt it. It's a twenty foot drop."

At this, certain her husband had been killed, the Countess fell in a swoon.

Lord Farron peered over the balustrade. "The Count has survived," he said dryly. "He's up and making for the woods. I can just make him out in the moonlight."

"He's limping badly, though," squinted Braider.

"I'll go after him," said Lord Farron grimly.

"And I," cried Braider. "By God, I'd no idea the fellow was such a cad."

"Go after him by all means," said the Duke hoarsely. "If I were not such a feeble old man I'd go with you. There's some pistols in the cabinet in my study. Take the stable boy along too – he knows the woods."

Lord Farron and Braider hurried from the room.

Edith and Charlotte meanwhile had raised the Countess's veil and were fanning her face with their hands.

"I think she is coming round," said Edith, as the Countess's eyes fluttered open. She gazed around in a daze.

"My...husband?" she asked tremulously.

"He is alive, madame," said the Duke carefully.

"Oh, thank God!" cried the Countess.

The Duke looked grave as he continued. "But I'm afraid I have to tell you that your husband ran into the woods and Lord Farron and Braider are pursuing him. He must be brought to justice."

The Countess nodded wearily. "I accept zis, monsieur. All I want is that he lives."

"You are tired, madame," said the Duchess. "I hope you will accept our hospitality tonight?"

"I shall be so glad," whispered the Countess.

"The story of how Lord Farron tracked you down," said the Duke, "and what led him to suspect the Count in the first place – must wait until his return."

Jeannie was summoned to show the Countess to one of the guest rooms.

"How can such a – genteel lady – be under the spell of that monster?" burst out the Duchess as the door closed behind her.

"We were all under his spell for a while," sighed the Duke. His eyes sought Sylvia's and she started as she saw the sorrow in them.

She had been so flooded with relief at her narrow escape, that she had momentarily forgotten what the whole debacle meant for her family. Now she remembered. There would be no money after all. The future was uncertain again.

At the same time it was clear that the Duke felt ashamed of the way in which he had allowed his wife and other daughters to pressurise Sylvia into marriage with a man who had turned out to be such a villain.

"I do declare," said the Duchess tearfully, "had I had the faintest inkling of his true character, I should never have encouraged our poor Sylvia to accept him."

The Duke regarded his wife in silence for a moment and then turned to Charity. "You will stay here tonight too, I hope?" he asked. "It is too late to journey home."

"Thank you, I should be glad to stay," accepted Charity gratefully.

"I suggest that you all retire," said the Duke. "I must wait up for Lord Farron. We will have to lock the Count in somewhere, until I can summon the authorities."

"*If* they catch him!" exclaimed the Duchess.

At these words, a chill wind seemed to enter the room and everyone in it shivered.

*

Sylvia went to her own room, where the emotions of the day so overwhelmed her that she fell asleep almost despite herself.

She had no idea how much time had passed, when she was awakened by a soft tapping at the door.

She sat up in alarm. "Come in!" she called.

She was relieved to see it was Charity.

"Has…your brother returned?" asked Sylvia tremulously.

Charity looked grim. "Yes, but without the Count. He and Braider decided to split up in the woods. The stable boy went with Braider but then – wanting I suppose to play the man – crept off on his own. Braider heard a cry and turned

154

back.

"The boy had encountered the Count, who struck him a blow that made him fall. When my brother met up with Braider and the boy, they were on their way back to the castle. The boy was crying because he had dropped his pistol in the struggle."

Sylvia was silent for a moment and then sighed. "What I cannot understand, Charity, is *why* the Count was so determined to marry me. We have no money and he certainly wasn't in love with me. So *why*?"

"I know the answer to that," said Charity carefully. "But it is my brother who has the full story. Will you allow him to enter and speak to you?"

"Of…course," replied Sylvia wonderingly. "Please help me into a dress and then I will receive him."

Charity complied and then went to the door.

It seemed Lord Farron had been waiting outside, for he entered immediately.

"I believe…you can throw some light on this…sorry affair," said Sylvia.

"Indeed I can!" said Lord Farron. "The story commences that night at the Count's lodgings. Do you remember a piece of cloth that lay on an open book of astronomy?"

Sylvia's eyes grew wide. "I..I do. It had…some kind of riddle written on it."

"Correct," asserted Lord Farron. "When I also read the name *Belham* on it, I was immediately suspicious of the Count. I decided to try and find out more about the cloth. Since it was almost certainly connected to the book of astronomy – the riddle contained astronomical allusions – the first step was to trace the owner of the book. The name on the bookplate, as you may remember, was Chagnon and the address Paris."

Sylvia gasped. "The Count's wife?"

Lord Farron nodded. "I went to Paris. I visited the house in the Rue Vieux Tolbiac and I found there – the Countess. She told me an interesting story.

"When your ancestor, James Duke of Belham, fled England during the Civil War, he enlisted with the French King's army, as you know. What you do not know is that his regiment was under the command of a certain – Louis de Chagnon."

Sylvia was speechless.

"The Duke was mortally wounded," continued Lord Farron, "during a skirmish with the King's protestant enemies led by the Prince de Condé. He lingered on in delirium for some days. Chagnon, who had become a friend, often visited him. One day the Duke pressed something into his hand. It was the cloth that had bound his head wound and the Duke had written on it in his own blood. He had written the very riddle I quoted to you.

"No doubt he intended to ask Chagnon to make sure this piece of cloth reached his family, but he died that very hour in Chagnon's arms. Chagnon thought the writing on the cloth was simply the result of delirium. Nevertheless he kept it, folded between the pages of an ancient astronomy book that the Duke had carried with him everywhere and which he also left with Chagnon.

"This book was deposited in the Chagnon library and the story of this unlikely friendship and its end entered Chagnon family legend, although knowledge of the actual whereabouts of the cloth faded from memory."

"And…how did it come into the possession of the Count?" asked Sylvia, perplexed.

"The Countess was married before," explained Lord Farron, "to a Chagnon. He was the last of the line. When he died his widow found herself reasonably well provided for, but even so, there were debts to be paid. She decided to sell part of the extensive Chagnon library and asked a friend if he knew of anyone desiring employment, who would help catalogue the books for her.

"Her friend suggested a gentleman he had recently encountered who was – shall we say – in embarrassed circumstances. The gentleman in question had inherited an estate but had gambled most of it away. He was at that moment in Paris and he needed money.

"That gentleman was Count von Brauer and he accepted Madame Chagnon's offer."

"And then he…married her?" cried Sylvia.

Lord Farron nodded grimly. "She had property, and an annual income, and he had nothing. He continued his work on the library after the marriage. Then suddenly, without a word to his new wife, he disappeared. Taking with him the astronomy book that the Duke had left to Louis de Chagnon all those years ago and, of course, the cloth that was folded between its pages."

"And…he knew what it was?" asked Sylvia faintly.

"Yes," said Lord Farron. "I believe he became acquainted with the history of the Belham family – and the legend of the treasure – at the gaming clubs on the Riviera."

"My father often tells the story," nodded Sylvia sadly.

"When the Count found the cloth," continued Lord Farron, "he knew exactly what it signified. He remembered that the present Duke of Belham had an unmarried daughter and decided to abandon his wife to pursue a greater fortune. He stole money belonging to his wife. He then travelled to England with the sole intention of marrying you and gaining access to the castle. You know the rest yourself."

"He used my poor father's gambling addiction to secure me," said Sylvia weakly.

Lord Farron looked at her sympathetically. "I'm

afraid so. And no doubt when the Count had the treasure in his grasp, he would have disappeared again!"

"Why have you come to me and not my father with all this?" asked Sylvia.

"I did not wish to raise his expectations when his health is not sound," said Lord Farron. "If the treasure exists, then all may be revealed to your family. If it does not, there is no disappointment. Except – except for you."

Sylvia drew herself up. "I could easily bear that," she said.

Lord Farron regarded her admiringly. "Good. So shall we start?"

"What!" exclaimed Sylvia. "N..now?"

"What better time?" asked Lord Farron.

Sylvia's face fell. "B..but we don't have the cloth. We don't have the riddle."

"Ah, but we do," smiled Lord Farron. He drew a piece of paper from his waistcoat pocket. "You obviously did not see me but I copied the riddle down."

"And…can you decipher it?"

"I believe so."

Sylvia looked at Charity and back to Lord Farron. "Then…let us begin," she said with a determined air.

Lord Farron bowed and unfolded the paper. "Here's the first line. *'A square within a greater O, below the one and then below.'* The square is the castle, the greater O is the sky. The castle is below the sky and – below the castle are – ?"

"The vaults!" exclaimed Sylvia. "The entrance is on the south side of the castle, near the stables."

As quietly as possible, though brimming with excitement, Sylvia followed Charity and Lord Farron down the stairs and out of the castle's main entrance. Soon they stood before two oak doors set at a slope low in the castle wall.

The vaults were not often entered and Lord Farron needed all his strength to heave them open by their iron rings.

Charity had brought a lantern. Lord Farron took it and led the way down the stairs.

At the bottom of the stairs four corridors led away in different directions.

Lord Farron read out the next clue.

"*The hand that's held against the sky, now directs the seeker's eye.*' Well, in ancient times, people put their hands up against the stars Castor and Pollux and the span between them was used as a measuring device for the rest of the night sky. Castor and Pollux are found in the north west, so I believe we take that north west corridor."

They set off. The beam from the lantern swung before them. The vaults had at one time been used for storage, particularly of wine and beer. Now it was empty, full of cobwebs and rotting casks.

They arrived at a corner where two corridors led off to the left and to the right.

"*His bootes towards the alpha's light, the path that follows must be right,*'" read out Lord Farron. "Well, the 'right' might not *mean* right. It could be a red herring. But in fact, 'bootes' is a star of which the alpha star is Arcturus, the pathfinder, and these both rise due east. And it is indeed the passage to the right that leads east."

Before moving off Lord Farron, noticed a rusty spade standing against the wall.

"This might come in useful," he mused. "I shall take it."

The three then walked quietly along the corridor. Set high in the wall at various intervals, under the ceiling of the vaults, were a series of small windows through which faint moonlight filtered.

Lord Farron held up his hand and his companions halted. He read out the next clue.

"*'Pause at the pane within the maze, under the growling dancer's gaze.'* The maze is the vaults, where one could indeed get lost." He looked around and then pointed.

"The pane we want – is there. For through it we can see – the star known as the 'bear' which people once believed 'danced' around the pole star."

Sylvia and Charity looked up in wonder. Lord Farron continued.

"*'Where an arctic glister all alone, illumines the last holy stone.'* Well, the arctic glister is the pole star itself. It too is visible through that tiny window."

He paused, his eye moving to the floor. "And see – how the light shines – straight onto that white stone there."

Sylvia and Charity regarded the stone.

"*'And there where prayers once were said, my earthly chattels found their bed.'*" read Lord Farron.

He looked thoughtfully at the stone. "I believe under that stone we will find what is called a 'priest's hole,' where the catholic clergy often hid from their persecutors. No doubt many fervent prayers were said there! And I suppose James, Duke of Belham did see it as the 'last' stone, for the catholic royalist cause was lost. I think we will find below – James, Duke of Belham's 'earthly chattels,' or – his treasure."

"How will we raise the stone?" asked Sylvia, trying to keep her voice steady.

"That is where this spade will come in useful!" said Lord Farron. "The edge is sharp and thin, and there is a gap between that stone there and the next."

Sylvia and Charity watched as he manoeuvred the

spade into the gap and started to push.

The stone creaked as it shifted. Sylvia held her breath. Suddenly she turned her head.

What was that noise behind her in the corridor? It had sounded like a footfall.

"What's the matter?" asked Charity.

"I thought I heard something."

The three waited, listening. But there was no other sound, save the faint drip, drip of water on stone.

"Sounds as if there's a pane open somewhere," said Lord Farron.

He resumed his task. Sylvia and Charity gasped as the stone finally rose. Lord Farron pushed it back.

He picked up the lantern and swung it over the gaping hole that was revealed.

Its beam was met with the glitter of gold and precious stones.

"We are saved!" cried Sylvia, clasping her hands to her breast. "My family is saved."

"You have done my work for me. Excellent!" came an all too familiar and chilling voice from the shadows.

The Count stepped forward. In his hands was a pistol – the very pistol that the stable boy had dropped in the woods.

Lord Farron cursed as he saw it.

In his other hand the Count carried a sack. He now threw this at Lord Farron.

"Fill it," he ordered. "Fill it with – the 'chattels' you have found here!"

"You won't get away with this," growled Lord Farron, tensing for a move.

"You think not?" said the Count. With a sudden lunge he was at Sylvia's side, the pistol pointed at her neck. Lord

161

Farron froze.

"You do see," shouted the Count, "that you must obey me now?"

His jaw set, Lord Farron opened the sack and began to shovel in the gold and jewels that lay in the hole.

"Help him!" gestured the Count to Charity. She hastened to her brother's side.

Sylvia could smell the wax on the Count's moustache, stale and malodorous. She clenched her fists, wishing she could strike out at him.

When the sack was as full as it could be, Lord Farron hoisted it and threw it across to where the Count stood.

"There, villain," he said bitterly. "Take your – spoils of deceit – and go."

"Not without Lady Sylvia," grinned the Count. "Do you think I'm a fool? She will be my hostage. If you attempt to follow me – she is dead."

He began to back away from Lord Farron and Charity, the heavy sack in one hand, the pistol still at Sylvia's neck, forcing her to move with him. Lord Farron watched desperately.

"I will follow you to the ends of the earth if you harm her!" he cried.

"Then I must be rid of you now!" snarled the Count.

For one second, the pistol was turned away from Sylvia and raised towards Lord Farron. With a cry she grabbed at the Count's wrist with both hands. The pistol wavered.

"Get away, you fool," shrieked the Count.

Lord Farron took his chance. He leapt like lightning across the floor. Sylvia was knocked aside. She fell to her knees as the two men struggled above her. Then – there was a report. It shattered the silence of the vault, echoing from wall to wall.

The Count tumbled to the floor. Sylvia and Charity stared in horror as his blood seeped out across the cold, white stones.

*

Sounds of merriment rose from windows far below the tower roof, where Lord Farron and Sylvia stood in the moonlight.

The Belham family had come to dine at Farron Towers, along with Braider. Braider had explained – his eyes flickering again and again towards Charity as he did so – that he had hardly known the Count and had been surprised to be asked to officiate as Best Man at his wedding. He hoped he would now be judged on his own merits.

Charity had blushed under his glances.

The Duchess was resplendent in a shimmering new gown, with one of the necklaces discovered in the castle vaults gleaming about her neck. Charity was wearing a ruby brooch that Sylvia had given her from the treasure.

The Duke had recovered fully from his illness. He was so ashamed of the way in which his behaviour had almost led to the terrible sacrifice of his favourite daughter, that he had firmly turned his back on the gaming tables. All he wished for now was his daughter's happiness.

The Count, to everyone's surprise, had survived his injury. He was in prison, awaiting sentence. The Countess von Brauer had vowed that on his release – in some three or four years time – she would be waiting for him in Paris.

The Count's establishment at Endecott, financed with the money he had stolen from his wife, had been broken up. Polly had not found employment with the new tenant and was now a serving wench at a hostelry in Norwich, much to her chagrin.

Sylvia thought of all this as she stood in the moonlight, gazing over the estuary towards Endecott. Tears of relief started in her eyes at the thought that she would never have to see the Count again!

Lord Farron followed her gaze. "You know," he said teasingly, "it's a mystery to me how that fellow the Count had two such lovely ladies vying for his attention!"

Sylvia, stung, burst into tears. "I…did not…want his attention, sir," she sobbed. "I only wanted…to save my poor father…from the disgrace of bankruptcy."

Lord Farron gently lifted her chin. A soft breeze stirred the curls on her forehead as her brimming eyes met his.

"I suspected as much," he murmured. "Do you think, if I had believed for one moment that you truly loved him, I would have kept this token of you?"

To Sylvia's wonder, he held up the white and gold mask she had worn all that time ago at Lady Lambourne's ball.

"And do you think," continued Lord Farron, "that if I had believed you wanted nothing more than to be his wife, I would have ventured so much to save you?"

Sylvia shook her head, stifling her tears. "I..I do not know, sir."

"Then know it now," said Lord Farron. "I only wanted to hear it from your own lips. Lips that now belong to no other man, lips that I, at last, may kiss."

He bent his head to hers and Sylvia's heart took flight within her breast as she gazed up at him.

"Now that you may be mine, my darling," breathed Lord Farron. "Demand of me what you will and you shall have it. Even if you desire the very stars in the sky!"

With a sigh of happiness, Sylvia yielded herself, body and soul to his lips……